Russian ice capade

The RPG erupted, and the river ice beneath Track's horse shuddered and began to crack. The powerful animal reared, and Track slid from the saddle as the horse stumbled into a wide fissure that had opened in the ice. The cold water gripped the horse in a cruel vise, squeezing a terrified scream from its throat.

Track rolled across the ice toward the animal, tearing at the heavy bags that were lashed to the saddle. The horse screamed again as it thrashed in the freezing water. Track reached under his parka and tore his Walter P-5 from its holster. Then he pumped the 9mm twice, sending two mercy slugs into the horse's brain.

He looked up to see a Russian scout car bearing down on him. As he lay on the ice, he brought the Walther on line with the men clinging to the car's sides and fired. One man spun away from the speeding vehicle, bounced once and then slid across the ice.

Machine-gun fire hammered out a return message, lashing Track's face with sharp diamonds of frozen water. Track was prone on an ever-narrowing peninsula of ice, and the ice was cracking beneath him with every breath he took.

Now available in the exciting new series
from Gold Eagle Books

TRACK

by Jerry Ahern

TRACK
Certain Blood

JERRY AHERN

A GOLD EAGLE BOOK FROM
WORLDWIDE

TORONTO · NEW YORK · LONDON · PARIS
AMSTERDAM · STOCKHOLM · HAMBURG
ATHENS · MILAN · TOKYO · SYDNEY

For Laverne and Anthony—
happiness. . . .

First edition April 1985

ISBN 0-373-62006-3

Printed in Canada

1

His thighs were stiff with the cold, and as he looked down at the shivering horse beneath him, Dan Track could see the ice-encrusted fringe of his mustache. His frozen hands moved slowly, and as he clasped them more tightly to the reins that curled over the heavily padded pommel of the crude saddle, he thought they were going to break. He was living a nightmare. It was cold, real cold. The thick, sheet ice that covered the river he was crossing was slick and treacherous. The mountains surrounding him had the aura of jagged crystal. The cold was deep inside him, and he could feel his stomach cramping with it.

He glanced at the SPAS-12 that hung from its sling, stock collapsed, beneath his right arm. It was coated with a thin film of ice. To touch the metal with a bare hand would mean tearing your flesh apart when you took your hand away.

Dan Track moved his legs, urging the small Asian horse ahead. He shrugged his shoulders deeper into the gray woolen blanket wrapped around his head, shoulders and back, but it did him no good. Despite the thermal underwear, despite the heavy, black, woolen knit shirt, despite the crew-neck sweater over that, and the V-neck sweater over that, and the hooded arctic parka over that—he was cold. His ears were warm, though. Not the warmth that comes with true freezing, when the body gives up to the mind and the danger signals finally stop like some sort of alarm clock run down. His ears were actually warm. He wore a navy wool watch cap, and wrapped over that, beneath the hood, a woolen scarf that not only covered his ears and neck but swathed his face just below his frozen mustache. He focused his attention inward on the pleasant warmth of his ears, his eyes serving as sensors only, squinted against the razor-edged wind, to watch what of the caravan there was ahead of him.

One of the camels in front of him was growing stubborn, stopping. Mechanically, Track reined back, slowing his horse. He had given the horse a name he could pronounce. Since its mane was very gray, he had named it after someone whose mane was also very gray—Sir Abner Chesterton, his liaison with the Consortium of International Insurance Underwriters. But on this mission, Track was working for no one but himself; his soul was his employer.

One of the Kirghiz tribesmen accompanying him dismounted and nearly skated across the creaking river ice to urge the camel ahead.

Track turned his head slowly, not wanting to dislodge the blanket, and looked around.

In 1333, in the writings of the medieval traveler Ibn Battutah, the mountains that surrounded him had been named Hindu Killer, likely a bastardization of Hinhu-Koh, meaning Indian Mountains. Track favored the former sobriquet—the Hindu Kush *was* a killer, a patient killer because time was inevitably on its side.

One thousand miles long, two hundred miles wide, the mountains were cold and formidable.

He almost felt sorry for the Russians, whose occasional patrols lurked in the mountains.

The camel, after vomiting at the Kirghiz tribesman and missing, seemed in a more agreeable mood and started ahead.

"Come on, Abner," Track muttered, nudging his knees against the animal, the ice beneath them creaking ominously. They were still a good two hundred yards from the ice-coated rocks of the far riverbank, and he forced himself to ignore the creaking of the ice as he had ignored it before. It was that or be constantly terrified.

But he was terrified. The camels made their own traction with the squishing action of their hooves. But the horses were shod, and when the ice became perilous, the horsemen would dip low and forward to sprinkle sand that filled bags hanging from each side of the saddle in the paths of the horses to prevent them from slipping. The lead horseman began to do this now.

Track ran the edge of his tongue over his chapped and cracked lips. He shifted forward, partially losing the blanket, instantly colder, scooping a stiff-fingered handful of sand from the bag and sprinkling it ahead of his mount.

Rahman Mirza's horse was suddenly beside him and Track looked up from the dark, almost fecal-colored sand he spread before his own mount at the sparsely bearded, hawk-nosed yellowed face.

"You appear cold, Major Track." Rahman's English, Track had learned early on, was excellent—the man was vastly well-read and had spent two years living away from the mountains.

"Appearances are often deceiving, Rahman, but in this case the appearance is reality."

The Kirghiz chieftain laughed. "You ride well—that is to your advantage. To fight your animal would only make the travel much more difficult, I think."

Track shrugged. "But I do not ride as well as you, nor is my animal at all like yours," he said. Track had adopted the stilted, formalized English of Rahman out of courtesy and out of practicality, so that they would better understand each other. And there was formality to consider—the chieftain was among the most respected men of the Kirghiz.

"I have traveled a great deal, Major Track, and for a time I rode with the chopendoz and was one of their number. I won this beast after a great Buz-Kashi in which much blood was spilled."

The goat drag, Track thought—the national game of Afghanistan. "Blood of the dead goat or blood of men?'' Track asked, forcing a stiff smile across his frozen face.

Rahman laughed heartily. ''The blood of men. The goat is filled with sand and water. The blood of men is different.'' Rahman leaned down from the left side of his horse, a light gray, with a black mane and tail, and spread sand before Track's horse and then before his own. Track realized he had been paid an honor. As Rahman rose, Track dipped to his right, scooped up a handful of sand and sprinkled it before Rahman's horse and then before his own.

He glanced at the Kirghiz chieftain's face, the black eyes clear and unflinching shielded beneath the epicanthic lids. ''I shall miss your company, Major, when we cross the pass beyond the river.''

''And I will miss yours, Rahman.''

''Desiree Goth's agent, Faring-Brown, spoke of some vendetta that obsessed you.''

Track had never discussed the purpose of his journey with the Afghan—and it was not that the Kirghiz chieftain was actually asking him now that made him begin to talk. He thought absently that it might somehow warm him. ''Many years ago, my sister and her husband were supposedly killed in the crash of their automobile—''

''A horse is more reliable, Major.''

''But slower.''

''Not this horse. But I am being rude—''

''Apparently they weren't killed. Either they were kidnapped or went behind the Iron Curtain of their own choice. Somehow, my sister believes that I attempted to murder her and her husband and actually murdered their son, George."

As if no moral question was involved, the Kirghiz chieftain murmured, "So, you seek revenge."

"Her husband studied in these mountains and to the east, and learned how to manipulate the human mind. I think he has manipulated hers. I think he is a traitor to his country and helps the Russians."

"You go then to rescue your sister?"

"Yes."

"What of the boy?"

"George? A good friend, Sir Abner Chesterton, is keeping George busy so he doesn't find out about his parents."

"This George—he would want to come too, then, you fear."

"Yeah, and that wouldn't be good."

"You will kill your sister's husband?"

Track wanted a cigar, but didn't dare remove his gloves to get at one. "Very possibly. I don't know."

"This is very much trouble for a woman," Rahman said dismissively.

"Is there no woman you would risk danger for?" Track asked him pointedly, looking into Rahman's face as the Kirghiz chieftain rose after sprinkling sand before their horses. They were nearly at the riverbank. "Yes, if the Russians had my sister and did terrible things to her mind, I think perhaps I would feel as you do, and perhaps want to kill her husband, too. This boy— George?''

"George is twenty-six, so he's not a boy."

"What will he do when he learns of this?"

Track looked down to the ice and let some sand drift from between his gloved fingers. "Hate me. Maybe try to kill me."

"But you can tell him of these things, and surely—"

"How would you feel toward someone who wouldn't tell you that your dead mother may still be alive, and who may well kill your father?''

"I think you will be a lonely man, Dan Track. Allah has smiled on you that Desiree cares for you. At the least you will have somewhere to go where there is feeling. Some are not so fortunate as you. Where will the boy go?"

"To me, if he wants. He's been like a son to me."

"I think he will go to you to kill you—I sorrow for you, Major.''

"I think you're right," Track told him. The ground ahead seemed less slick, and the horses could move with more assurance as they picked their way up the rock escarpment that formed the riverbank.

"Faring-Brown has asked me to convey a message to you from Desiree."

"Now? At this precise moment?"

"Yes. I was to give it to you only when we had crossed the river and were about to breach the final pass and then travel down into the warmer lands beyond. I have memorized the message as I was requested to do."

"What was the message?" Track asked him.

"That she travels a different route to avoid your scorn. That she comes with the great Zulu, to meet you at the house of Hakim Mohammed, a Chinese house between the foothills and Khorog. From there, an airplane will take you three on your way."

Track didn't know what to say. She wasn't supposed to come, the mission would be dangerous, the chances for success small. The thought of her presence angered him, yet made him feel secure at the same time.

"I have met Desiree many times," Rahman continued. "She is not an ordinary woman, I think. She can ride, she can shoot, she can fight. And yet she is soft and beautiful as a woman should be."

"I'll pass along your comments. How could she get across the mountains?"

"Desiree has many friends among the Communist Chinese, friends whom she might well trust with her own fate and the fate of Zulu, but not with the fate of an American soldier."

"Ex-soldier," Track interrupted.

"One is never an ex-soldier, Major," Rahman Mirza stated. "There are some in China who work against the Russians, and Desiree has worked with them. Her face and the face of Zulu are known and trusted. Your face would not be. But the route that she will have taken is not a route of comfort—it is cold as it is here, and the horse trails are steep and ice slicked. She will long for your warmth as you will for hers." Rahman clapped Track on the right shoulder, with his five-pound ham-sized hand.

"Can you wait to take her back?" Track asked him.

"Desiree? Hardly, Major. But she is safe at the house of Hakim Mohammed. He is a trader and wealthy in a land where wealth is forbidden. But he can provide items the Russians have great difficulty obtaining, and so he is allowed to flourish in his Chinese house."

"Shit," Track snarled, watching the cloud of steam as it left his mouth. "She was safe in India."

"She is not a woman who relishes safety, Major. She is a rarity, and that is a great fortune for you."

"Yeah," Track said soullessly. "A great fortune. Desiree has just put herself in mortal danger for me. How fortunate, indeed." He was silent for a moment, then added, "You wait near the home of this Hakim Mohammed—get her out of there for me."

"And what, my friend, if Desiree does not wish to go?" Rahman adjusted his Tomaq, ice crystals falling from where the massive fur hat had met his forehead.

"Throw her across your saddle and take her away against her wishes, then. If I find my sister and her husband, if Robert is up to something—"

"All of hell will break open!" Rahman Mirza chimed in.

"All hell will break loose," Track corrected automatically as his attention was drawn to something happening in front of him.

He thought for a moment that one of the two camels carrying the Kirghiz tribesmen's belongings had lost its footing on the ice. The animal fell from right to left, blocking the narrow rocky trail leading up from the river.

Rahman reined in his Buz-Kashi horse, and Track heard the sound of steel against leather as Rahman pulled a revolver from beneath his cloak. It was a very old gun, and between the fingers of Rahman's gloved hand Track could see the yellowed ivory grips of a Smith & Wesson .44 Russian, a revolver from a century ago. The Buz-Kashi horse reared.

The point man shouted something Track could not understand.

"Kist?" Rahman called back.

Again the point man shouted something Track could not understand. Suddenly, as if in mid-sentence, the man's throat vomited a stream of blood and the tribesman tumbled from his horse.

Rahman fired his pistol into the rocks beyond

the riverbank as a chunk of ice was ripped from the ground near Track's horse. "*Zud boren!* Let's go!" Rahman shouted.

The second camel was punched in the head to move it aside, as the two remaining Kirghiz tribesmen wheeled their mounts and came toward Track in a rush. Track's right hand closed more quickly than he'd thought it could on the butt of the Walther P-5 secured in an outside pocket of his arctic parka. The trigger guard was just large enough for his gloved index finger to slip through, and he snapped the trigger back twice, firing into the rocks as his horse reared under him.

"*Zud boren,*" the Kirghiz chieftain shouted to Track, wheeling the Buz-Kashi horse, letting it spring from the icy rocks and over them and onto the river surface, the animal's hooves skidding uncontrollably, as it shrieked into the cold clear air. "Let's go quickly," Rahman Mirza shouted again in English.

Track brought his horse under control. He could see movement in the rocks, and detected the mountain uniforms of the Soviet special forces. The gunfire was now audible, and Track saw the second camel go down, blood splattered across its right side, a hideous wail issuing from its blubbery lips as it slipped on the icy rocks, sliding toward Track.

Track wheeled his horse and dug his heels into its flanks. The horse responded, and he was airborne, clearing the rock boundary that edged the riverbank. Then suddenly Track's stomach had a sinking feeling, and he was colder than he had felt an instant earlier.

His horse was going down.

Track jumped clear. His left foot caught for an agonizing second in the stirrup, and then he was free as the horse tumbled and skidded on the ice.

Track rolled to his feet, the Walther P-5 in his fist.

A Soviet trooper, armed with an AKS-74, was advancing on him. The Russian's rifle fired a burst of heavy metal, and Track threw himself to the ice, sliding along it toward the trooper, firing the P-5 until the slide locked open, empty.

The Soviet trooper staggered, then fell.

Track pushed himself up, catching his balance on the slick surface, and ran along the ice toward his horse.

He looked behind him once as he stabbed the empty and temporarily useless 9mm into his coat pocket. At least a dozen Soviet troopers were scampering down from the rocks. One of those who remained was shouldering a Dragunov sniper rifle.

Track dropped to his knees, skidding along the ice, twisting his body, bringing the SPAS-12 up from beneath his arm and shoving it forward. With stiff fingers, he clumsily worked the slide to charge the chamber. He let the slide fly forward, working off both safeties as he extended the twelve-gauge shotgun against its sling, tensioning it there.

He snapped his trigger finger back, and the rocks and ice near the sniper exploded as the high brass slug dumped its load—a miss. Track fired again, and the sniper's rifle fired skyward as the body rocked backward, the face all but disintegrated.

AKS-74s blazed from the rocks, their sound reverberating like a chorus of screams. Track was on his feet, running toward his horse.

Track reached for the animal, letting the SPAS fall to his side on its sling.

Suddenly Rahman was there, his mighty Buz-Kashi horse rearing as an AK-47 roared in his hands. "Hurry, my friend—hurry!"

Track knotted his left fist into the terrified animal's mane as the frightened horse slipped again, losing its footing, almost seeming to dance across the ice. As Track's foot found the stirrup, the horse shied away under a fresh volley of automatic-weapons fire.

Track's fist wrenched at the mane, and he threw himself up and forward, landing roughly half in the saddle. He snapped his heels against the horse's flanks and urged the animal forward.

There was a burst of assault-rifle fire and the ice behind Track's horse exploded as Rahman shot at the animal's heels. The horse flew forward, Track clinging to it with both hands as he positioned himself in the saddle.

Letting his weight fall forward over the horse's outstretched neck, Track looked beyond the animal's massive head and across the river ice. Steam snorted from the horse's nostrils and flecks of ice torn loose by the animal's thundering hooves pelted at Track's face.

Track looked back once, and caught sight of an all-terrain vehicle rolling down out of the rocks, crushing the bodies of the dead camels beneath it. Special forces troops clung to the machine, and a machine gun mounted on its roof started to open up.

Track looked away, molding his body to the animal under him, the shapes of the two other Kirghiz tribesmen growing in definition ahead of him as his horse darted forward.

Glancing to his left, he saw the figure of Rahman Mirza riding low in the saddle, his AK-47 at full extension pointed behind him. "Like the Buz-Kashi—ride for your life, Major," Rahman shouted.

And the horse was suddenly sprinting ahead.

Even as he urged the animal on, Track could sense the horse's unsteady footing. He played out the trailing ends of the reins into a quirt, and he worked it now against the horse's flanks, his heels digging in hard again and again. The animal was full out, low over the ice, the hooves seeming to barely touch the surface.

Track glanced back again. The ATV was coming up fast, machine gun slugs ripping massive chunks up from the ice behind Track's horse. "Aw, shit," Track snarled, bending low over the animal's neck again, the ice-encrusted mane stinging his face and neck.

The two Kirghiz tribesmen who had gone ahead were stopped near the center of the ice, and Track felt a smile cross his lips. Both of the men carried RPG-7V antitank rocket launchers strapped to their saddles.

Track glanced behind him again. The armored scout car was closing in, the machine gun turret twisting, the barrel elevating—he was no longer the target.

One of the RPGs fired, and beneath the roar Track felt the ice shudder and then heard a sickening crack. His horse reared and stumbled and Track skidded from the terrified animal, crashing to the ice as the horse tumbled through a widening break in the ice. As the powerful animal's head and neck plunged into the icy water, the horse let out an almost human scream.

Track rolled across the ice toward the frantic animal, as it struggled in the icy grip of the river. His left hand reached behind the cantle of the saddle, tearing the heavy felt saddlebags free as he rolled back. The horse was almost totally submerged now, his forelegs flailing uselessly against the ice, his large eyes wide with terror.

Track reached under his parka and awkwardly ripped a second Walther P-5 from an ill-fitting military holster. He pumped the 9mm twice into the horse's head, mercifully killing the animal rather than letting it suffer.

There was no time to mourn. The BRDM-2 scout car was still coming, crossing the water now that had opened before it.

Track lay on the ice, leveling the Walther toward the men clinging to the car's sides. He fired and dropped one man before a burst of machine gun fire ripped away more of the ice beside him. Track lay prone on an ever narrowing peninsula of ice, clutching the felt saddlebags. The P-5 was empty in his right fist, and there was no time to reach for the SPAS. The ice cracked beneath him with every breath he took.

He heard the whoosh of the rocket as the second RPG fired, and he covered his head with his hands. The amphibious BRDM-2 scout car was perilously close.

Then there was another roar, and Track felt a searing heat he no longer thought it was possible to feel. An instant later, the cold returned with an iron fist. When he looked up, the scout car was gone, disappeared into the river. But a half dozen of the Soviet troopers ran across the ice toward him, their AKS-74s firing.

Track heard Rahman shout off to his left. "Major! Here!"

Fifteen feet of plaited leather snaked through the air toward him. Track reached out for the bullwhip with his left hand, closing his fingers around the wide fall at the tip.

He was being dragged, the ice beneath him breaking up, collapsing under his weight as Rahman's Buz-Kashi steed powered away. Track skidded along solid ice now, gunfire hammering toward him as he released the whip. He rolled from the momentum of being dragged, and came up on his knees, the SPAS extended against its sling, his finger snapping back against the trigger. The SPAS roared again and again, joining the heavy chatter of Rahman's AK-47. One of the Soviet troopers went down, followed by another and another until the last Russian gun was silenced.

The SPAS was empty and Track stood to his full height, groping for spare shells in the pocket of his parka, loading them up the tube as he started forward across the ice. "Major," Rahman shouted. "We must get out of this place—it is no longer safe to be here!"

Track glanced over his shoulders as he loaded the remaining four rounds into the tube and began to work the magazine cutoff to squeeze in the ninth double O buck. "Thanks for saving my life—twice, unless I missed something."

Rahman Mirza only nodded, then shouted to his two men who were mounting up a short distance. *"Inja khub nist! Zud boren!"* He looked back to Track. "My animal can easily carry us both, my friend. But we must ride quickly; the Russians will certainly be on the alert for us now."

Track grabbed the felt saddlebags, planted his foot in a stirrup, and swung up behind the Kirghiz chieftain. Track thought the mountain warrior was a world-class master of understatement as he muttered under his breath, "They will certainly be on alert for us now. . . .".

2

Sir Abner Chesterton lit one of his infrequent cigarettes, inhaling deeply from it as he stood beside his horse. He had ridden to the hunt as a boy, but had never liked it. He had enjoyed the riding, but the yelping of hounds trailing a fox had always sounded like a death moan to him, and he had considered the Englishman's hunting of the fox barbaric and cruel, the unspeakable in pursuit of the uneatable. His father had not agreed.

He watched the smoke curl upward on the slight, chill wind—it was really the first serious disagreement he had had with his father, the first of several. His father had saved a commission in his regiment for him at the beginning of the war against Hitler, a safe clerking job. But instead, Chesterton had signed on with the Royal Commandos, later finding he was among their youngest members. His father had not spoken to him for a year afterward, but then, after his return from some particularly deadly business in France, the old man had broken from a crowd of officers, walked up to him and embraced him.

His father died two years later in North Africa.

It was then that Sir Abner assumed the hereditary title and learned his father had spent too much time fox hunting and too little time attending to the family affairs. Chesterton had managed to save their country home, but little else. After the war, he moved into the British S.I.S., a natural offshoot of his gallant but necessarily anonymous service in the commandos.

Now he was with the Consortium, and he wondered if he was just clerking again. There was evil in the world and except for a few times with Track and George, he had fought it with nothing more dramatic than a checkbook that wasn't even his.

He had never married. There had been women, and even at what he considered his advanced age, there still were. But none could replace a girl who had died during the war. After the girl had died, he had fought the Germans harder, killed when there was sometimes less than a need to do so.

He dropped the cigarette to the ground, grinding it out under the heel of his combat boot.

He turned to watch George Beegh, talking in Pidgin English with the Turkoman leader. He wondered what this trip—if they survived it—would do to George.

Though Dan Track had never said it, it seemed implicit that if George's father, Robert Beegh, was a traitor to his country and had harmed George's mother, Track would somehow take care of it.

Chesterton felt that George realized that—hence his sense of urgency. Once orphaned, he did not wish to be orphaned again—even by a half measure.

George turned away from Maradan, the Turkoman chief, and walked back from the lip of the rise, burying his hands in his coat pockets. His black Jack Daniels baseball cap was pulled low over his forehead, his pencil-thin mustache nearly overshadowed by the growth of beard from not having shaved for ten days.

"What did he say, George?" Chesterton asked as George walked up to him.

"His scout reports that the village is clear of Russians," George said as he opened his coat and reached under it to his right hip. A Colt Government Model .45 appeared in his right hand and he worked the slide back, letting it run forward, leaving the hammer cocked, upping the safety to lock it. "But just in case." The younger man grinned.

"Yes, just in case." Chesterton patted the shoulder holster under his Navy P-Coat. His stainless Walther PPK/S was there as it should be. He opened the P-Coat, reaching to the small of his back for the FN/Browning GP, lifting it from its hidden holster and turning it over in his gloved hands. "Tell me, George, what good will pistols and a few assault rifles do against Soviet troops—I really want to know."

"Look, Sir Abner, you shouldn't have—"

"Shouldn't have come?" Chesterton interrupted. "Really, dear boy. How was I not to come? You are my friend, as is your uncle—"

"Dan should have told me—"

"But he didn't—and out of love, out of no other motive—"

"He still should have told me," George insisted.

"Perhaps, but then that's second-guessing another human being, isn't it? And since each of us is so terribly different, we're rather doomed from the start, wouldn't you say?" But Chesterton didn't wait for an answer. "We all do what we think is best in this life, George, for whatever reason, good or evil. I think your uncle's motivation was the best possible sort, and if you were to sit down for a moment and appraise his actions rationally rather than emotionally, you would find yourself in agreement with me."

"Look, I know you and Dan are friends. And I know you're trying to help—"

"And the important thing," Chesterton said as he replaced the Browning, "is that he is your friend as well. You've always seemed to me to be more than uncle and nephew—good friends, the best of friends, men united by a common bond. If you lose that chasing after a ghost from your past, I'm afraid you'll lose something that is irreplaceable."

"Why don't you quit the insurance business," George snapped, "and start doing the sermonettes on TV at night?" George looked away for a moment, then turned back and grinned. "Look, I'm sorry, Sir Abner...I, ah...."

"Actually, George, I've recently given some thought to quitting the insurance business, as you put it. But only time will tell. It looks as though Maradan is ready to travel on. Shall we?" Chesterton didn't wait for an answer, swinging up easily into the saddle, settling himself as George walked toward his horse. George mounted, secured his M-16 to the saddle by thongs mounted near the pommel, then moved out.

Chesterton fell into the procession and found himself riding beside Maradan's chief lieutenant as they started down out of the snowy foothills and toward the snow-splotched, muddy basin in which the town rested. Chesterton decided on conversation with Maradan's lieutenant. "Is the weather this cold here throughout the winter?"

"Yes."

"Ah, I imagine it breeds a hearty race, this sort of climate."

"Yes."

"I see. Have you a wife?"

"Yes."

"And children as well?"

"Yes."

"Fortunate you are, old boy. What are their names—the children, I should say?"

"Yes."

"Yes?"

"Yes." Maradan's dirty-faced, turban-clad lieutenant grinned broadly, what few teeth he had yellowed and dismally alone in the cavernous blackness of his mouth.

"Have you always been such a singular linguist, then?"

"Yes."

"Ah, I see."

"Yes."

Chesterton merely nodded, saying nothing else at the moment.

Their horses rounded an outcrop of snow-streaked gray granite and Chesterton could see the village in as great a definition as he had seen it earlier through the binoculars. Flat-roofed stone huts, the roofs pitched forward against the rain, were clustered together in an unplanned layout.

A solitary narrow bridge traversed the expanse of river that bisected the village, and as the procession started across it, Chesterton scratched at his beard, hoping there would be enough hot water for a shave and a bath. He had found himself grateful for the wind and the cold. It prevented him smelling himself and the men with him.

He kept riding, watching George just ahead of him.

As if George could sense him doing that, he turned, twisting in his saddle, calling back, "Maradan said it would be half an hour until we were nice and warm in the village and eating some hot food."

"What sort of hot food?" Chesterton asked. But George just shrugged and turned away and

Chesterton didn't press the matter. Whatever it was, shy of a few obvious things, he would eat it.

Black-faced karakul sheep dominated the edge of the street leading into the village, and as the men rode through them the sheep bleated in protest, but parted in a wave along both sides of the brown muddy road. Their smell was overpowering, Chesterton thought.

They passed an old man dressed in long robes. His white beard seemed to grow directly out of his gray turban. The camel the villager led tried nipping at Chesterton's horse, and then at Chesterton's right thigh, but Chesterton edged his animal away quickly. He glanced back at the old man—the old man's face was impassive.

As they rode on, the street widened into what was evidently a town square of some kind. Merchants and craftsmen ringed all sides, hawking their wares or manufacturing new ones—rugs, small statues, ornate-looking knives. One shop caught and held Chesterton's attention. An out-of-place glass display case housed an assortment of pistols and heaps of loose ammunition. He eyed the pistols as they rode by—a Browning, like his own, a Colt revolver with pearl-handled grips, a Luger with a long barrel and an assortment of modern revolvers that by their look he branded cheap. They were haphazardly arranged with various pieces of other guns.

The village was too passive, Chesterton thought. He had arrived as a foreigner in many strange villages in stranger parts of the world than this, and there was always some commotion. Where were the children, the beggars, the more aggressive sellers?

He settled his left hand on the pommel of his saddle, and moved his right hand across his abdomen, closing his gloved fingers loosely on the butt of his Browning Hi-Power.

"Anything strike you as a bit odd, George?" he said.

"Yeah, real odd. You too?"

"Quite. And just in case, I make the best route out of here the way we came in."

"Agreed." George nodded, looking back once, then looking away. He had loosened his M-16 from his saddle and it now rested across his lap.

Very slowly, Chesterton withdrew the Browning Hi-Power from his waistband, his right fist gripped tightly on the butt, his left hand, still fully gloved, working back the slide, then letting it run forward to chamber the first of the 115-grain JHPs. He left the hammer up at full stand, and raised the thumb safety.

Chesterton's eyes drifted right and left, stopping on a smiling face beneath a cream-colored turban—the man sat on an ornate rug and stared. But something about the smile seemed terribly wrong to Chesterton. "Maradan—let's get out of here," Chesterton called forward.

The tall, lean Turkoman twisted in the saddle. The look on his face was very similar to that on the face of the old man sitting on the red rug. "George! Run for it," Chesterton shouted, reigning back on his horse. As the animal reared, he heard clicking sounds, one after the other in ragged succession.

He knew the sound well. He had been captured by the Germans once, and had been marched into a courtyard at the crack of dawn each morning and stood before a firing squad—just to say good-morning with a dash of terror. The sound he heard now was like that sound from decades ago—the working of bolts for automatic weapons.

To his right, a child shielding each of them, were six Soviet special forces troopers.

To his left stood six more, again using juvenile shields.

"George, don't do anything," Chesterton shouted.

Chesterton looked back, still holding his Hi-Power at the ready. He could see Maradan still smiling. He looked at George. George was staring at the riverbed, where a wooden door had opened near the base of a building perhaps fifty yards along the river course. There was some type of recoilless rifle there, and tied in front of it, positioned as if in crucifixion, was a child, a little girl.

Chesterton lowered his weapon. If the recoilless rifle was fired, the first round would shred her body to bloody fibers. Slowly, the pistol clenched in his right fist, Chesterton raised his hands in the air above him.

He watched as George threw his M-16 into the river and clasped both hands behind his head.

And Maradan was still smiling. . . .

STRIP-SEARCHED AND DRESSED again, Chesterton ran his long fingers through his thinning hair as he exited the hut, squinting in the gray sunlight. He was cold again, and automatically started to button his P-Coat.

George marched beside him. Two Soviet soldiers flanked them on either side, while two more marched in front and two guarded the rear.

Chesterton shook his head, studying the gravel and mud over which he walked, only half listening as George muttered, "These assholes don't speak English—back me up when I make my play."

Chesterton realized that would be suicidal, but likely suicide would be preferable to what the Soviet troops had planned at any event. "Of course, George. Been rather good knowing you, by the way."

"Same here, Sir Abner. Just be ready."

Chesterton only nodded, looking up finally and assessing their surroundings. There were at least two dozen Russians, including two officers, all of them heavily armed. Their faces were unkind faces, dirty, haggard, disgusted faces, the mouths slits that would allow anger to pass through them. He walked on, pushing his fingers through his hair again. Suicide would be far preferable, he thought.

The two troopers in front of them stopped very suddenly, and Chesterton found himself plowing into the lead man. It reminded him sickeningly of the marches each morning to the mock firing squads, never knowing if this was the day the firing squad would be for real or not.

He looked up. Sitting on Chesterton's own horse was a Soviet officer, a huge furry chopka low over the man's eyes, the earflaps down, a red star set at the center of the front flap. Chesterton shrugged his shoulders—he'd always admired men who died with a smile on their lips. "Lovely day, isn't it, comrade?" he said to the man.

The Russian did not smile. "You are English?" he asked.

"Yes, as a matter of fact—and Her Majesty's Government should be most distressed to learn that myself and another innocent traveler have been set upon by your men."

"You are Chesterton, then," he said, mispronouncing the name a little. Otherwise his English was very good, Chesterton thought.

"How do you know my name?"

The Russian officer seemed to ignore what Chesterton said, and turned to George. "And you are the American named Beegh." It was not a question but a statement, and he pronounced George's last name like "beech."

"Yeah," George answered. "And the United States Government's going to be pretty pissed too. Who the hell are you?"

Chesterton thought, Bravo, George, but said nothing.

"I am Major Constantin Fierienko, and both of you will accompany me to my headquarters."

"For what purpose, Major? I demand to know," Chesterton said with force.

Fierienko looked at Chesterton. "You," he said, "can demand nothing. The one Beegh is the one we seek. We have orders to bring him to headquarters alive. That you live, Englishman, is sheer accident."

"I see," Chesterton said diffidently.

"What the hell's so special about me?" George snapped.

"I only follow orders. Personally, I would have shot you both." Chesterton didn't watch the major as he spoke, but instead watched Maradan and his men. Maradan still smiled, but his right hand was slipping to his heavy gray coat and beneath it.

Chesterton bit his lower lip, then decided to keep talking. "Whose orders are those, Major? Can we at least be told that?"

The Russian officer shrugged, the horse moving under him as he did. "They come from KGB headquarters in Moscow, Englishman."

"My, my, I hadn't thought we were that important," Chesterton said as he smiled. He glanced past the major to Maradan—he thought he saw a pistol butt. Then he looked very quickly at George. "Had you thought we were that important, George?"

"No—no, I hadn't," George replied, nodding. "Hey," George continued, turning to the Russian. "What's the KGB want a couple of innocent tourists for, anyway? I want to talk with the American embassy."

"There is no American embassy."

"Fine, then put in a call to Washington for me," George demanded. The Russian repeated what George said, Chesterton knowing enough Russian to follow the drift of the major's words. Suddenly there was laughter from the major, the other officers and the enlisted men with their AKMs still trained on Chesterton and on George.

The laughter stopped abruptly as a single pistol shot rang out and the front of the major's head exploded. Chesterton threw his arms around his horse's neck and bulldogged it to the ground. As the major's body tumbled from the saddle, Chesterton's right hand grabbed for the man's belt—his own pistol was there and Chesterton's right fist closed over it, his bare flesh feeling the contact of the cold metal. He swung onto his horse as it started to stand, and prayed the major had left the pistol chamber loaded. Chesterton pulled the trigger as the horse righted itself and reared, killing one of the armed guards nearest to him. George was already locked in combat with three men.

Gunfire was all around them now. Maradan's husky voice shouted something Chesterton couldn't understand—but it sounded like a battle cry.

Chesterton made to fire at a Russian soldier near him, but one of Maradan's men snapped the Russian's head back and ran a sickle-shaped knife across the soldier's throat from left to right, spraying blood everywhere.

Chesterton's horse reared again, and he rode into a knot of Soviet troopers, his Walther PPK/S discharging again and again, his right foot lashing out into the face of another officer. As the man's head snapped up, Chesterton fired out his pistol into the man's face and chest. The Russian collapsed in a heap in the mud.

Chesterton could see George taking on four of the Russians in hand-to-hand combat, and he charged his horse into the five of them. The horse shouldered aside two of the Russians, and Chesterton threw his body—he was too old for this, he told himself—over the other two, dragging them to the ground through sheer momentum. His left hand caught on the face of one of the Russians, and as they rolled across the rocks and mud, Chesterton crossed the man's jaw with his right fist.

The Russian's head sagged back, his tongue lolling from the mouth, but Chesterton hit the man again, the base of his palm contacting the base of the Russian's nose, breaking the bone, driving it up and through the ethmoid bone and into the brain. Chesterton rose from the straddling position he had taken over the man, searching the ground for a weapon.

George was twisting the head of one of the Russian soldiers like a madman trying to free a cork from a bottle of wine. There was a loud crack, and the Russian's body went limp, the head hanging at an odd angle to the neck as George let the body fall to the mud.

Chesterton found his weapon—an AKM. He set the selector to full auto and sprayed, hosing a concentration of a half dozen of the Russians. There was more gunfire from both sides of him now, but there wasn't time to find the source.

Two Russians went down, then a third and a fourth. The last two started to raise their hands in surrender and Chesterton edged the pressure off the trigger of the AKM. But the gunfire on both sides of him erupted anew, and the last two Russians went down.

Chesterton wheeled to his right. Maradan stood staring at him, a submachine gun in his hands.

"No prisoners," Maradan remarked casually, lighting a cigarette.

"What the bloody hell is going on here, Maradan?" Chesterton growled.

"Know the Russians want you two American fellows. We think, get Russian soldier in village and kill Russian soldier. Very simple, okay?"

It was George who said it. "Fuck you!" Chesterton heard George say, and then George started laughing and for some reason Chesterton couldn't understand, he started laughing as well.…

THEY HAD RIDDEN in silence for a while after helping Maradan incinerate the bodies of the Russians.

But riding beside Chesterton now, as they ascended into the foothills of the Hindu Kush, George began to speak. "Why would the KGB know about us?"

"Food for thought, certainly," Chesterton answered.

"What do you mean by that?"

"If they know your name and my name, either one of two things has happened. They may have captured your uncle and used drugs to force him to talk. But that's hardly likely since he was expecting that I would keep you occupied in the States while he was off settling family business."

"What's the other possibility?"

The tack of the horses clinked a little, making a pleasant tinkling sound against the creak of the leather of their saddles and the clopping of their hooves on the rocky mountain pathway. "The other possibility, George?" Chesterton cleared his throat. "The other possibility, quite frankly, is that your parents—one or both of them—are working with the Russians or in some other way were made to give some information. But just how they would have known you were coming is something I'll confess would baffle me. But it really doesn't matter a damn, does it? They know we are coming and the reception committee we just met won't be the last looking for us. What frightens me, speaking plainly, is that for some reason they want you alive. And that frightens me a great deal.''

Chesterton urged his horse ahead—he didn't want to talk to George at all just now.

3

The room was very dark, and he used her real name. "Diane—tell me what you see."

Her eyelids fluttered in the beam light from his penlight, and he clicked it off, feeling the darkness as warm around them, hearing only her breathing. It was even, soft, as it was at night when they slept.

"Robert?"

"Yes, Diane, it's Robert again. Do you see our little boy?"

"But he's not little anymore, Robert. He's big." She laughed softly in the darkness. "Bigger than you or Dan. He's very tall and strong."

"That's good, Diane. But where do you see him?"

"He's riding a horse. It's very cold there—I can feel that. Very cold." There was a subtle clicking sound as her teeth chattered. He had made her too good, he realized, had realized from the start. The drugs he had used had broadened her consciousness to the point where she felt what she "saw," and it was perhaps that, as much as the drugs, that had destroyed her.

"Where is George?" he pressed. "Is he with anyone now?"

"The same man, a handsome older man. But the older man is riding ahead of him. George looks wearier than he did when he was riding before."

"Perhaps he endured some trauma. We must know where he is, Diane, so we can bring him home to us. Where is he?"

"There are rocks and snow all around him, and he seems so terribly cold—I want to make him warm, Robert."

"You can, Diane. All we have to do is get him here with us and away from those bad men he is with."

"The older man doesn't seem bad—I don't feel that he's bad, Robert." Her voice was unsteady and in the warm stillness and the dark he could see her shaking slightly. He would have given her his sweater, but with physical contact she might lose what she saw.

"Where is he? Reach inside him. He knows where he is, Diane. Reach inside George and tell me."

"He's afraid, Robert, and he's confused. He's thinking about me! Oh, Robert, he's thinking such terrible things about you, Robert. George— George! Don't! Robert is your—please, George!"

"Where is he?" Robert coaxed. "The only way we can help him is to bring him to us."

"He's thinking about Dan now, Robert. He

doesn't know whom to trust. Robert—please!''
She began to cry. As the years had gone by, she had
become less and less stable a medium to utilize. The
visit with the doctors in Moscow had proved fruit-
less—they could not probe her subconscious as
deeply as he could with the drugs. It was only a matter of time until she was beyond reaching.

He pushed harder. "He is with evil men. Dan
has told him lies about us, and so has that older
man. We have to help George before it is too late.
Do you want him to die, Diane?''

"No!" She shrieked the word.

"Then you must find out exactly where he is.
Go into him and find out so we can send some of
our friends to get him for us.''

"Why can't we get him ourselves, Robert? I
want to hold George—Robert.''

"We can't leave here. It would be too dangerous. But we can get George here with us, and
everything will be fine—he'll be with you again.''
There was truth in that. If the drugs had worked
so well with her, they would work as well with
George. "Tell me where he is so we can rescue
him—or do you want your son dead, Diane?''

"No, no. He's talking with another man.
There's a caravan—very many camels, Robert—
from Mazar-e-Sharif, the man with the turban
told him, Robert. He—''

"When will they meet the caravan?''

"The man with the turban—''

"When will they meet the caravan?''

"Two days if they ride hard."

"Then I have him." He touched the remote-control light switch beside him in his chair and the room became suddenly very bright. Diane's eyes were wide open, staring and glassy. He picked up the second hypodermic and daubed the alcohol-soaked cotton ball over the inside of her elbow and injected her again with a drug that would make her sleep, and forget that she had been Diane Beegh again for a short while.

He closed her eyes with his fingertips and walked to his desk. Sitting down, he lifted the receiver of his telephone, telling the secretary, "Call this number for me in Moscow—very quickly."

He held the line—the drugs worked less well each time. Perhaps George could be his next medium.

4

The Kirghiz chieftain called a rest and Dan Track shifted down from behind Rahman Mirza, standing beside the Buz-Kashi horse as Mirza handed down the felt saddlebags that contained Track's few extra clothes, his spare pair of boots and the bulk of his spare ammo.

Track took them and worked his way up into the rocks away from the wind, as Mirza dismounted. Track sat on the flattest rock he could find and was instantly colder.

"Major, there will be Russians everywhere, I think. We had best be very careful," Mirza said as he walked up to Track.

"How soon until we reach Khorog?"

"And the Chinese house of Hakim Mohammed?" Rahman Mirza added, letting out a hearty laugh.

"Yes, and Desiree," Track conceded as he smiled.

Mirza shrugged. "Within two days of hard riding if we do not have to travel in circles to evade our Russians."

"And if we do travel in circles?"

"The will of Allah," Rahman Mirza said, raising his palms upward to the gray sky that seemed heavy with snow. "We shall eat—a small fire can be risked," he announced suddenly. There was no wood, but the fire would be of camel dung, Track knew—the other two riders with them carried large bags of it slung from their saddles.

THE FIRE STANK. Steam rose from it as the accumulated moisture in the fresh patties of camel dung evaporated upward over the pot in which the goat meat, wild onions and bread-dough noodles warmed. Goat meat and onions, when not mixed with the burning odor of the camel dung, have a heavy, pleasantly gamy smell.

"How will you leave Russian territory, Major?" Rahman asked as if picking up a conversation just dropped. But none of them had spoken since building the fire and huddling around its warmth. From the mouth of the small cave all four of them could see the barren landscape behind them, so no sentry was posted. And Rahman had contended that not even the Russians would be insane enough to come at them out of the pass through which they would soon travel. The winds were too strong.

So they merely sat, and Dan Track looked at Rahman Mirza's yellow face beneath the fur of the Tomaq and said flatly, "I don't know. Desiree gave me a contact in the city where I'm going, and said that the contact would know the way." He had not told Rahman Mirza that his destination was Alma Ata. It was a city about two hundred miles from the Chinese border, and one of the most secure cities in the Soviet Union. Alma Ata meant "full of apples," and the city was indeed full, boasting missile installations, a very large and formidable Communist party leadership and a top-flight scientific and industrial complex. Desiree had described it as a modern and beautiful city. She had been there on business. Very cosmopolitan, she had told him. He laughed at the thought—anything would be cosmopolitan after this barren and frigid wilderness.

"Let us hope that none of this has changed, Major," Mirza said after a moment.

Track had not told Rahman Mirza because he considered his destination on a need-to-know basis. Only Desiree, of necessity, and Sir Abner Chesterton had known it. If Mirza did not know the destination, Mirza could not be tortured into divulging it. The thought made Track colder still, but then Mirza signaled to the nearer of his two men and the man removed the stew from the fire and began ladling it into wooden bowls. Track accepted a bowl and one of the wooden spoons, and began to eat silently. The smell of the food had made him realize how hungry he really was.

Mirza spoke as he ate. "What do you think of my horse, Major?"

"He's a fine animal. You must be proud to ride him."

"Indeed, it is true. A fine animal—the finest of the fine animals of the Buz-Kashi."

Since Rahman Mirza evidently wanted to talk, and since it would take his mind from how little food there was and how very cold he was, Track asked, "How are Buz-Kashi horses selected?"

"They are not selected, my friend—they are raised for Buz-Kashi. Would you like that I tell to you how?"

"Yes—yes." Track nodded, trying to summon up interest.

"Very well then." Then he said something in his own language and one of the men—the one who had ladled out the stew—murmured something that sounded like approval. Then Rahman Mirza turned to Track and set down his bowl of food. Track mentally shrugged, setting down his bowl as well. This was evidently very serious to talk of the Buz-Kashi.

"In the very large cities the game of Buz-Kashi is not so good, I think, for there are teams that play against one another. But in the villages, every rider rides for himself alone, and the game is much more violent and faster and yet it lasts perhaps longer. A goat is beheaded, and then its insides are removed and the carcass is packed with sand and soaked in water to increase the weight—sometimes they weigh as much as a ten-year-old child or a small woman. The *hallah* circle—the circle of justice—is drawn and the game begins. Each man rides for the headless goat and fights to possess it or to take it away from another. This builds character, and will and endurance. But the Buz-Kashi horse is born to the Buz-Kashi. When the mare is in foal she is fed at least ten fresh eggs each day. When the foal is born, he is caught and prevented from falling to the ground. He is a strong foal and his wings must be guarded.''

"Wings?"

"The Buz-Kashi horse will fly." Rahman grinned, his cavernous mouth revealing his sparsely placed yellow teeth. "The horse is let to run free for three years before a saddle or bridle is used, before the animal is familiarized with the weight of a man. When the animal reaches the age of five years, it is rationed corn or melon with salt, and in the summer of that year put out into the heat and the wind, to build a tolerance for suffering, for the pain the animal must soon endure. To strengthen the horse."

"They look Arabian, the wide foreheads—" Track began.

"Ah, but they are special. Stronger than any ordinary Arabian, any ordinary horse. Faster than the wind."

"Your horse is a fine animal," Track concluded.

"The very finest. In your language, his name would be Wings of Dawn."

Track started to say something, but he saw Rahman Mirza turn his face away quickly and look skyward.

Track followed his gaze, seeing nothing, then

hearing a sound he had known was inevitable—the beating of helicopter rotor blades against bitter cold air.

"Russians!" Rahman Mirza exclaimed. Track grabbed up his wooden bowl, shoving the rest of the food into his mouth with the spoon—the next meal might be a long time coming. Tossing down the empty bowl and grabbing up his saddlebags and his SPAS-12, he started running down from the rocks in the wake of Rahman Mirza and his two men.

Mirza outdistanced his men to the horses and snatched up his saddle from the ground, throwing the blanket across the horse's back, followed by the saddle.

He was in the saddle, and let down his left hand. Track grasped it above the wrist, swinging up behind him. The helicopter sounds were louder now, and two gunships, Hind-As from the look of them, were coming in low. Their 12.7mm guns opened up, rock chips and chunks of ice blasting skyward, ripped from the living rock of the mountains around them.

"To the pass!" Rahman Mirza shouted as the big horse leaped forward. The horse skidded into a right-angle turn and vaulted into the rocks, finding footing where Track would have thought there was none.

Track glanced behind to see a blast of machine gun fire blow one of Rahman's men from the back of his horse. The riderless horse reared, then ran in pursuit of Mirza's mount and the second Kirghiz. Rahman Mirza ordered his horse forward, and the animal hurdled a low rock wall and then raced ahead.

Track looked forward, past Rahman Mirza's massive shoulders, to the approaching pass. The pass took the form of a tunnel, perhaps a hundred feet high, chiseled out of the rock by what force of nature Track could not guess.

The riderless mount was even with them now, and Mirza shouted to Track over the slipstream, "Take Muli's mount, Major!"

Track was already reaching for the mane and the pommel. The felt saddlebags were slung over his right shoulder, and the SPAS-12 hammered at his right side. He leaped, his abdomen taking the force of the pommel like a punch, and the wind rushed from him, but he swung his left leg over the animal's back and eased himself forward to settle into the saddle, hugging his knees to the animal. The Soviet helicopters were closing. Another blast of machine gun fire and the second Kirghiz seemed to erupt from his saddle, his body sailing skyward, the horse falling, skidding forward on the icy rocks on its knees, blood spurting from its throat, vomit from its mouth.

Track found the stirrups and dug in his heels. Rahman Mirza was riding low in the saddle ahead of him, firing out his AK-47 toward the choppers.

Track looked behind him again, the SPAS-12 extended, tensioned against its sling.

He fired toward the nearer Hind-A, and the helicopter swerved wildly away. Track knew that the best he could hope for was cosmetic damage, considering the range and the double O buck loads.

Track worked the trigger again and dug in his heels. The pass was less than two hundred yards ahead, and Track hugged his body against the horse to provide a lower profile as he glanced back again. Both of the helicopters were drawing back, one peppering the rocks with machine gun fire, the second hovering as men rappelled from the sides of the machine—Soviet special forces troops in mountain camouflage, AKS-74s slung to their backs. Track swung the SPAS-12 toward them, emptying the magazine tube, working the trigger as quickly as he could. He expected little success, but one of the Soviet troopers hesitated on his rappeling rope, then his hands and arms spread-eagled from his sides and he skidded along the length of the rope and slammed into the ground. Track let the SPAS fall to his side on its sling and rode hard.

Ahead of him at the mouth of the pass was Rahman Mirza, his AK-47 firing in short 3-round bursts, his horse rock-steady under him. Track heard Rahman urge him forward.

Track dug in his heels, keeping low under the level of the tribesman's fire, then suddenly reining in his mount as a burst of automatic-weapons fire sliced across the mouth of the pass. Track's horse whined loudly and collapsed beneath him. Track threw himself clear of the saddle, coming down hard against the rock floor of the pass. His right hip ached as he pushed himself to his feet and hugged the far wall, loading the SPAS-12 with alternating slug loads and shot shells.

Mirza's horse raced into the tunnel, its rider clinging desperately to the horse's mane. Track looked up to see that Rahman Mirza's face was a sickly gray.

Track reached out and dragged the huge Kirghiz chieftain from the saddle, easing him to the ground. Then he grabbed Rahman Mirza's AK-47 and leveled it at the advancing Soviet troopers, firing a long burst toward them.

The men tucked down, flanking the rocky pathway leading toward the cave mouth.

Track pulled back, dropping to one knee beside Mirza. "Where'd they—" he began. But there was no need to ask. Rahman Mirza opened his eyes and moved his left hand from his abdomen—the hand was sticky with blood and intestine.

"Like the goat, they have disemboweled me, my friend."

"Shit," Track snarled, putting down the AK, unclipping the sling from the SPAS in order to turn out the folded buttstock. Track shouldered the SPAS. The first load up was buckshot.

The Soviets were advancing in fire and maneuver elements, the rocks near Track's head fragmenting under the impact of their fire. Rock dust,

rock chips and spicules of ice powdered Track as
he fired. The shot shell caught the nearest man of
the maneuver element in the chest and abdomen,
hurtling the man's body back against another of
his comrades. A scream issued from his wide-open
mouth.

As the men of the maneuver element scrambled
for cover, Track fired again and a Federal super-
slug gouged a brick-size chunk of granite from the
wall beside the nearest of the troopers. The fire
element responded by blanketing the rock face of
the cave with autofire as Track ducked back.

Track picked up Rahman's AK-47 and stabbed
it around the corner of the cave mouth, firing
blindly downward toward the Soviet position.
Then he tucked back beside Rahman Mirza again.
Mirza coughed and blood sprayed from his
mouth. "You. . . you must ride from the cave and
into the pass, Major."

"Bullshit! We leave, we leave together, Rahman."

"We cannot leave together. If I move of my
own accord my intestines will spill from my body,
Major. I have seen many men die. You have, too.
We both know the face of death."

"Fine, I'll take the horse, but only after—"
Track didn't say the word.

"There will be no time then, Major. The Russians cannot find you in the pass of the winds because there are many small tunnels and some of
them are known only to the Kirghiz. Give my

horse his head and he will lead you into the right tunnel and out again. It is very narrow, very dark and very cold because the wind lashes at you. You must cover your ears against it, and cover the ears of the horse or you will both be deaf. Take him, give him his head.''

"No—"

"Draw me to the edge of the cave so I can shoot my pistol. Take the AK-47. Spare magazines are in my saddlebags. I have my pistol and my knife— I'll hold them as I die, and then cheat them of victory. In the Buz-Kashi, the goat is placed in the circle of justice. This,'' he said, indicating the mouth of the cave, "is my circle of justice.'' Rahman Mirza shouted something to his horse, and the big animal trotted up, lowering its broad head and nuzzling Mirza's face. Mirza seemed almost to coo to it as he spoke in his own tongue. Then he turned back to Track. "I have told him that you are his master now, to carry you well. He will obey you, protect you—"

"Rahman, I—" Track began. His mouth was very dry, and he noticed he could no longer feel the cold. Perhaps it was the anger, perhaps the danger—perhaps the friendship of the dying Kirghiz chieftain. Track reached up to stroke the forehead of the animal Mirza had just given him, and the big gray snorted.

"To the cave mouth, my friend,'' Mirza whispered hoarsely, coughing up more blood.

Track said nothing as he dragged Mirza toward

the cave mouth, easing him into cover. Taking the antique Smith & Wesson from the flap holster at Rahman Mirza's belt, Track pressed the revolver into the dying man's hand, but Mirza settled it on his lap.

Track knew the words Rahman rasped now—common phrases among the Afghans.

"Manda nabashi." May you not be tired. *"Zenda bashi."* May you live long.

Track placed his right hand over his heart, murmuring, *"As-Salam Aleikum."* Peace be upon you. There was no need to help Rahman Mirza with his pistol, for the Kirghiz chieftain, blood trickling from the left corner of his mouth, his eyes closed, was quietly dead. Under his breath, as the gunfire was mounting from outside, Track murmured, *"As-Salam Aleikum—manda nabashi,* my friend,'' and rose to his full height.

Track picked up his saddlebags and the AK-47, slinging the bags over the pommel of the saddle, and the AK under his left arm opposite the SPAS. He swung up onto the big horse's back, feeling the power of the animal beneath him. He nudged the horse slightly with his heels, and it sprang ahead.

He barely held the reins, his fate rested in following the words of Rahman Mirza—to give the horse its head. As he ducked to avoid low-hanging rocks in the cave ceiling, he began searching his pockets for things to use to protect his ears and the ears of the horse from the howl of the winds.

5

Dan Track was into the tunnel of the winds, the scarf that had shielded his own face now wound through the bridle of Mirza's horse to shield the animal's ears as best as possible. Track wondered how much protection it offered, for his own ears were more heavily swathed in a knit watch cap and the hood of the parka, and they ached with the whistling roar of the wind blowing from beyond the mountains. The horse had led him through the cave and to the nexus of a series of rock passageways. Without pausing, the animal took the passageway second from the extreme left and moved along it. But the passageway had suddenly and drastically begun to narrow and Track could no longer keep his feet in the stirrups, instead drawing his legs up and squatting cross-legged and precariously in the saddle. But the confining walls so close to him at least allowed him to restore his balance when he would slip from the saddle to one side or the other.

And it was totally dark.

Behind him, he could hear the shouts of the Soviet troopers. They had swept past the dead body of Rahman Mirza, Track knew, and now followed the sounds of the hoofbeats in their pursuit of him.

There was not room enough to turn around and fire at them if they got that close, and in the darkness he would have only been making himself a target.

His horse moved slowly, and the sounds of the men behind him indicated that they ran quickly.

The special forces would be well equipped, prepared for every contingency. They would have powerful flashlights.

And even if he kept ahead of them, although the horse could outdistance them easily once the tunnel reached its end, the helicopters could have crossed the mountains and be waiting to intercept him.

Track's animal moved ahead.

The wind's howling grew in intensity, like maddening voices shrieking unintelligible obscenities, he thought. The noise was beyond hearing—he felt it inside him.

Soon the sound of the horse's hooves would be obscured totally by the shrieking of the air rushing through the tunnel. Even now, Track could barely hear the occasional shouts of the troopers behind him.

He held the SPAS-12, the buttstock folded down, vertically in front of him between his body and the neck of the horse. He held the AK-47 the same way. The tunnel seemed somehow to be still narrowing, and the wind, beyond its demonic volume, was bitterly cold. His face and an exposed portion of his left wrist where the storm sleeve of his parka and his gloves no longer met were numb.

The Buz-Kashi horse kept moving.

Track could no longer hear the sounds of his pursuers.

Perhaps the horse had taken the wrong tunnel, and this tunnel would simply become progressively narrower until the animal would be hopelessly lodged in it and Track would be trapped between the horse and the Soviet troopers behind him. Track tried to make the thought go away.

He refocused his mind on Desiree. She would be waiting for him at Hakim Mohammed's house near Khorog. But as much as he wanted her for his own needs, he did not want her there. She was not safe there. The Russians were searching for him and they would not stop once he had crossed beyond the mountains. There would be more Soviet security the closer he came to Alma Ata. He wondered if Baslovitch had anticipated this and warned the KGB. He did not blame the Soviet KGB major if he had. Track had been caught totally offguard when Baslovitch had come to him in Switzerland and divulged that Diane and Robert Beegh were still perhaps alive. He could not expect Baslovitch to fail in his duty to his own country and not alert security forces that he, Track, might be coming to Alma Ata.

Track suddenly started to lose his balance. The

tunnel was widening dramatically, and Track shifted his stiff, sore legs down and rammed his feet into the stirrups. The total darkness persisted, and he clung to the neck of the horse, the SPAS shifted back quickly on its sling to ride beneath his right arm, the AK slung beneath his left.

There was a sense of falling, of weightlessness. The totality of the darkness was disorienting him.

Dan Track could do nothing but hold on to the animal beneath him, unable to even see the animal.

Suddenly there was light. Track's eyes squinted as he shot a glance behind him. A high-intensity flashlight was neutralizing the darkness.

The roar of the wind, greater than it had been, obscured all sound.

From the edge of the darkness past the light he saw a muzzle-flash, then a series of muzzle-flashes. He felt something rip at his coat, at the hood of his parka, and the big horse shuddered beneath him and increased the pace.

Track swung the SPAS-12 behind him, working off the quick-employment safety and twitching his index finger against the trigger, firing the alternating slug and buckshot loads toward the light. There was a wild burst of muzzle-flashes in the darkness behind the light, then another. The light wavered. Track felt the subtle change in the rush of air past his face, and he knew that a bullet had just missed him. He fired out the SPAS, unable to hear it over the wind. The light wavered again, and he saw a body fall in silhouette past it and the light shatter. Darkness.

Behind him, they were still firing, but Track did not look back. He could feel the rock dust and chips of granite spray in the air as he rode on.

He dug his knees into the sides of the horse and the Buz-Kashi seemed to heighten its speed.

Ahead of him, he saw light.

It was gray and dim and his horse charged toward it.

Track edged the AK-47 forward on its sling, blindly working off the rifle's safety, ready to go down shooting.

The magnificent horse was picking up speed, and now in the shafts of gray light, Dan Track could see the shadows of the rocks around him, the shadows like something unreal. As he and the animal he rode moved through the shafts of light, he ducked low across the animal's neck, ready.

The light grew in intensity.

Dan Track squinted against it.

He suddenly realized the howl of the wind had subsided, and above it he heard the drumming of his animal's hooves against the stone floor of the tunnel, the tunnel once again widening into a cave.

He could faintly hear the popping noises of the Soviet assault rifles from behind him. And yet his hearing was dominated by the crashing-wave sounds that reverberated inside him and would be doing so until his hearing recovered.

The gray light appeared stronger now, and the

shafts of light were bands of bright, fuzzy, light-diffusing smoke. The horse quickened its pace.

Track clenched the AK-47 tighter in his left hand.

The horse vaulted upward as Track clung to the animal's mane. Track's body shuddered as the animal's hooves came down. The gray light was blindingly bright and washed over him—they were outside the tunnel.

Track glanced back only once. The Soviet troopers were racing after him, at least a half dozen of them.

One of them raised something that looked like a hand-held radio. Track doubted it would work in the mountains. But he pointed the AK-47 behind him at arm's length and fired a 3-round burst, then another and another. The radio man went down, the radio exploding into what seemed like a thousand pieces of plastic. Track let the empty AK-47 fall to his left side and knotted both fists into the horse's mane.

No helicopters were in the air above him now.

Only the ragged gunfire thundering over the crashing-wave sounds that already filled his ears was of immediate danger.

Abandoning the reins, hugging his frame to the animal he rode, Dan Track urged the big horse ahead.

TRACK HAD BATHED the animal's hooves in a rag into which Track had urinated. Urine was sterile and warm enough not to freeze on the animal's flesh. He sat now on some rocks in the mouth of a small cave, miles beyond the tunnel and Soviet soldiers who had pursued him.

He judged it would be another day and a half before he reached the Chinese house at Khorog.

Snow fell heavily beyond the mouth of the cave. If helicopters still searched for him, their task would be nearly impossible without the most highly sophisticated electronic equipment.

The SPAS-12 was freshly loaded with shot shells.

The AK-47's spent magazine was reloaded with fresh rounds from Rahman Mirza's saddlebags. Track mourned the death of the man. Too many men like Rahman Mirza had died fighting Russian communism. The Russians could be contained to a degree, but only to a degree. Soviet communism was like a cancer. It would inexorably and unavoidably spread. Many more good men were destined to die.

The horse stirred beside him, and Track reached up and stroked the animal's forehead as it bowed toward him.

Too many good things were going.

If his sister was alive, she had likely already been destroyed by the Russians in one way or another. She had been deprived of seeing George finish growing into a man, deprived of the pride of knowing her son had done well. She was one of millions of victims.

Track had left the U.S. Army C.I.D. before retirement because the evil he had combated had finally got to him and sickened him. He had only reluctantly joined the Consortium in the fight against international terrorism and major crime. It had been an alliance with the Consortium or George's neck. And the old feelings of disgust had returned quickly. He remembered Johannes Krieger, the insane Nazi who had tried to seize the world through the threat of thermonuclear holocaust. How little things had changed. Genocide survived under another name, on a grander scale.

Violence, betrayal, deceit and evil were everywhere.

Track thought about taking the easy way out—marry Desiree and live with her away from the evil forever. But could he really accept Desiree's line of work and feel easy about where her money came from?

An idea grew in him.

A man working from the inside could probably do so much. Track spoke Russian well, though he could not read it. Desiree's smuggling network supplied Soviet dissident resistance—she could supply his needs. And he wouldn't last that long against the might of Soviet communism's core to require all that much.

To join with the Afghan *mujahedeen* was only to strike out at the symptoms, not the root cause of the sickness.

The idea intrigued him. Attack the KGB, the Soviet power base, but attack it from within.

Show them they were not safe in their citadels built on human misery and inhuman depravity.

Dan Track snipped the end of one of his cigars, lighting it in the blue yellow flame of his Zippo.

He wondered how the Cuban cigars brought into the Soviet Union for the high-ranking party officials and the KGB leadership would taste.

Dan Track decided he would find out.

6

The car he had stolen had died a miserable death from lack of nourishment coupled with exhaustion—out of gasoline and a broken fan belt. The fan belt he could have fixed, Baslovitch thought, staring at the machine in the roadside ditch, the rear wheels embedded in a snowbank. The snow had come very early to Russia this year. The gasoline was beyond help.

With his gloved hands, he scooped snow and began burying the car in the snowbank.

It was the third automobile he'd stolen since fleeing Moscow, and the poorest of the lot. But it was imperative that he reach Omsk. It was there that the few things he had placed away over the years were hidden, things that he needed to be able to reach Alma Ata and intercept Dan Track and then to utilize Track's escape route. Since his visit with Track in Switzerland to tell his friend about his sister, Baslovitch was a wanted man. Having escaped an execution attempt at his Moscow apartment, he was a man on the run with very few places to run to.

The first order of business was to get off the

road, he told himself, cataloging his next moves as he heaped snow upon the stolen car. He had always worn gloves in the cars he had stolen, and purposely not smoked in them so no telltale bit of ash could be linked to him and then traced along a string of stolen vehicles. Contrary to the Soviet government's official position, auto theft and other types of miscellaneous crime were no rarity in the Soviet Union. The mere fact of cars being stolen would not lead inevitably to him. At least not right away.

He kept heaping on the snow. After leaving the road, he must find shelter. Night was coming soon, and with it more snow. He could survive a night in the snow without the benefit of shelter, but it would deplete his meager stock of food—bachelors who were poor cooks habitually kept little in their apartments.

Shelter was the first priority.

Otherwise, an American Hershey bar, a few cigarettes, a few mouthfuls of vodka and a vitamin pill and sleep.

The snow heaped over the useless car, he turned his attention to the broad open field beside the road. Windswept snow drove across it in clouds of white against the gray sky.

He jumped the small embankment of snow, walking in it now, grateful for the cowboy boots he had elected to wear. They were low heeled enough that he could walk easily and comfortably in them, and the sides were high and kept the snow off his feet and ankles. The leather repelled moisture and kept his feet dry.

But they were not exactly warm.

He kept walking, the wind blowing his lined trench coat against his legs as he bent against its force.

His ears were cold and he hunched lower in the collar of the trench coat, walking ahead against the wind.

There was a sudden stillness as the wind dropped. Large flakes of new snow brushed his face, falling so rapidly that they seemed to form a curtain surrounding him.

He tried to run, before the snow became so heavy he could not see the edge of the field. He couldn't risk losing his sense of direction. Ahead of him he saw a house and a barn, and he ran toward them, stumbling in the deep snow and the pothole beneath it, catching himself as his mouth filled with snow, then running on.

He could not be seen from the farmhouse—of that he was sure. The snow would obscure him. He saw no light, could not discern if there was smoke from the chimney. If the farmhouse was abandoned, as many of the privately owned farms had been, it would be all the better.

Sergei Baslovitch kept moving, the snow whipping wildly at him as the wind picked up again. He could barely see. He had heard of men freezing to death in a sudden blizzard such as this, freezing to death when they were only yards from life-saving shelter.

He stumbled, the surface feeling different beneath the snow. He moved ahead, then suddenly a dark shape loomed up ahead of him.

He sagged against it, feeling his way along its length. His face brushed against some cold glass for an instant. He kept edging along the dark object and suddenly there was a shaft of yellow light.

A woman's voice called out, the voice old and cracking. "Who are you?"

Baslovitch staggered toward the door. "I am a traveler, Comrade. I need shelter." He was too tired to lie and the truth made a better story, however unspecific. "My car broke down some distance from here. I was starting for this farmhouse, and then the snow caught me."

"I cannot let you freeze, Comrade—come inside." Baslovitch lurched toward the broad beam of yellow light and half fell through the doorway, his stuff bag banging hard against the rough wood of the floor. A sudden light-headedness overtook him as he swayed on his hands and knees for a moment. Snow melted from his eyebrows, and great crusts of it fell from his hair and across his forehead. "You are ill?" he heard the woman ask.

"I am just very cold, Comrade," he told her. Which was true. "Forgive my rudeness." Baslovitch made to stand up, but he sagged instead against the side of an old rocking chair. The yellow light was intensely bright, and he saw that it came from a fireplace on the far wall of the small farmhouse.

"Tea?" the woman asked.

"Yes, Comrade, tea would be magnificent."

"Take off your coat, the snow will only soak through into your clothes."

"Yes, thank you." Baslovitch struggled to his feet, unsteady with the sudden flush of warmth. The car had been cold, the short trek across the field colder. He slipped the stuff sack from his left shoulder and let it sag to the floor beside him, unbuttoned the trench coat and shrugged it off.

Baslovitch looked for a place to put it, but the old woman took the coat from his hands. "I will take this, Comrade," she said, adding, "Why don't you sit down, before you fall down."

"Thank you," he whispered, settling into the rocking chair.

"By the fire. Bring it closer by the fire, Comrade," he heard her call from behind a heavy faded curtain.

Baslovitch stood, drawing the rocking chair closer to the fire, the fire looking piteously small on closer inspection. "I must thank you, Comrade. You are very kind, especially to a stranger," he called out.

The woman did not answer, but brought out a pot of tea and a single cup on a chipped wooden tray. The china had once been very good, he realized. A small plate that matched the cup and saucer held two slices of dark bread. "Eat this," she told him. He could tell that she once had a son, the way she had so easily fallen into the pattern of command.

She poured from the pot, and Baslovitch took the cup and saucer from her, sipping at the tea. It was very hot and very weak. She was poor, he realized.

"What is your name?" she asked.

There was no point in lying—if the KGB tracked him this far, his description with a false name would be just as damning. "Sergei," he told her, but not giving his last name. Honesty was one thing, stupidity quite another.

"I knew a man named Sergei once. He was tall and strong like you are. Have you traveled far?"

"Yes, Comrade, very far, and I still have a great deal of distance to travel." He took a slice of the bread—it was stale.

"It is all I have," she said, motioning to the bread plate. "And forget 'comrade.' I am Mariana Antonova."

Baslovitch nodded as he set down his teacup on the floor between the rocking chair and the hearth. He placed his stuff bag on his lap and worked the zipper open.

He extracted the two remaining Hershey bars and the bottle of vodka. Sergei Baslovitch looked at the old woman and she laughed. . . .

THE WIND HOWLED outside, and Baslovitch's hair was still wet from going back into the storm and chopping a meager supply of firewood, but the fire was warmer now and the old woman would have enough wood to see her through several days after he was gone.

Beyond asking his name, she had left him alone. But now she stared at him and said, "You have a gun in your bag, and you run from the police, do you not?"

Baslovitch laughed. "The police should hire you, Mariana Antonova. You are very perceptive."

"Who are you, Sergei?"

Baslovitch sipped at his vodka, then lit a cigarette. "I am a man who did a very foolish thing. I tried to help a friend."

"Would you do it again?"

Baslovitch laughed. "That is the foolish part of it—I would, all of it. It was a matter of honor—you would understand that," he said as he looked into her eyes.

"Do you have a young lady?"

"I suppose that I do," and he thought of Tatiana. For an instant he was afraid for her that somehow she might be linked to him. But she would be safe in Academgorodok. Or would she? "Yes, very pretty, very young—too young for me. I may never see her again."

"Do you really believe that?"

"No, I will see her again. Somehow, I will see her again."

"Where do you run to, or are you too busy just

running?'' Mariana Antonova smiled, sipping at her vodka.

"No, I know where I am going. But I cannot tell you. I have already told you more than it is good for you to know. If the KGB should follow me—"

"What will they do to me?" she said as she shrugged her shoulders. "I am very old. I have an illness. They have forced my husband into his grave and my son into his, hounding them to give up the farm. They will not allow me to sell my vegetables in the market at Omsk. They sentence me to death even now. They cannot kill me twice. But you are young—"

"But years are reckoned by what one has done, not the years alone."

"You are a policeman," the old woman said. "I could always tell a policeman. During the Revolution, I helped my father and I could tell a policeman for him then. I would call out to him through a little whistle and a tube and tell him that the police were near. I have never lost the ability."

"My boots are too shiny," Baslovitch said as he laughed. They were not shiny at all—stuffed with rags, they were as near the fire as he dared put them without letting them crack. He would oil them before he put them on.

"They are not made in Russia, I can tell that," the woman continued. "And I saw a watch like yours many years ago on the wrist of an army officer."

He glanced down at his wrist.

"The knit tie you wear is silk. The jacket and the coat are from England or America. I recognize the writing—my father spoke some English."

Baslovitch stood, a little drunkenly since he'd had little food and a great deal of vodka, and snapped his cigarette into the fire. "And the cigarette is American," the old woman said as she smiled.

He had been smoking a Lucky.

He drew himself to his full height, watching her pale-blue eyes in the firelight. "I am undone, Madame Comrade," he began. "May I present myself? Major Sergei Nicolai Baslovitch, Committee for State Security of the Soviet, Retired." He laughed as he bowed formally to her.

He sat down, before he fell down. "Do not repeat my name to anyone," he said in a warning voice. "It could cost you your life."

"The doctor at the state clinic has been forbidden to treat me because my papers have been canceled. But he treats me anyway. I have heart trouble. I have had three heart attacks, and I will die very soon. Your secret is safe with me, Major Sergei Nicolai Baslovitch," she said, then added the word, "Retired."

She stood, and Baslovitch rose impulsively as she did. "My father was tall and strong, like you," she told him. Then she whispered good-night and disappeared behind the curtain. . . .

IN THE MORNING, Baslovitch looked behind the curtain and saw that she was still breathing.

He left her the last chocolate bar and the remaining half of the bottle of vodka. He left her all the money in his pockets. There was more money where he was going. And if he needed money on the way, there was always some commissar with padded pockets from whom he could steal it.

And he left her a note. It said simply, "Until we meet again."

With his boots freshly oiled and his coat buttoned to the neck, Sergei Baslovitch stepped out into the snow.

7

George Beegh shifted his weight in the saddle. His tailbone hurt. As a little boy, like most little boys, he reflected, he had passed through the inevitable stage of wanting to grow up to be a cowboy, riding the mythical range with a sixgun on each hip.

But he had been riding day in and day out for many days now, and the charm of the childhood fantasy was wearing thin.

Maradan sat astride the big bay beside him and suddenly murmured, "It has been too easy, I think, since leaving the village."

George shifted his shoulders under the parka. He was still damp and cold from sleeping out on the rocks. "Are you thinking of using Sir Abner and me as bait again?" George said as the tall, lean Turkoman turned to face him.

"There was no choice. But no more."

George nodded.

In the valley below, he could see the caravan— about two dozen camels, a dozen horses and a half dozen burros.

"We ride to meet the caravan," Maradan proclaimed as he raised his right arm to signal to his half dozen men, then started his horse down the rise and toward the floor of the valley.

George reined back, fighting his mount a little as the animal wanted to follow Maradan's horse. In a moment, Sir Abner Chesterton was beside him. George felt in brighter spirits, saying to Chesterton, "You know, for an old guy you did all right in the village."

"Thank you for such a wonderful compliment, George. We'll make a diplomat of you yet."

"I mean it. Dan told me about the time you spent in the commandos, but ridin' a desk all these years—"

"Handball, swimming. And then, of course, whenever I'm in London the Blackpool Fireballs."

"The what pool what's?"

"Blackpool Fireballs—my cricket club. Remind me to tell you about it. And I don't consider fifty-nine that horribly old, George. And neither will you when you age a bit."

George shook his head, then guided his horse down the slope.

Ahead, he could see the caravan starting to slow as Maradan rode up to it, standing in his stirrups, waving his rifle in his right hand, discharging a round as if giving some sort of signal.

The camels came to a halt, and the point animal dropped to its knees. A turbaned man dismounted easily and walked toward Maradan. George heeled his horse, urging it ahead.

He watched as Maradan dismounted. The camel rider and Maradan were approaching each other on foot now, exchanging flourishing salaams. George started reigning in, and the horse beneath him broke into a slow trot. Chesterton had stopped some distance to the left side of Maradan, his horse's off foreleg pawing nervously at the sandy ground.

Maradan's six riders had fanned out along the caravan's length as Maradan and the camel rider spoke.

George could hear their words as he settled his animal beside Chesterton's, but understood nothing, the language was totally alien to him.

Chesterton, as if reading his thoughts, leaned right in the saddle, turning to George and saying, "I can follow some of it. Maradan, I gather, is recounting some of the trouble we had in the village—they've just had a good laugh over it."

"Wonderful." George nodded, pulling the peak of his Jack Daniels baseball cap lower over his eyes. The sun was still working its way to its zenith, and because the sky was largely cloudless over the valley the light seemed very bright. "And these guys are going to get us to Alma Ata?"

"Only near it. We'll be disguised as members of the caravan. After that we're on our own."

"How am I going to look like an Afghan?"

"A turban, a robe. You're a bit tall, but even a crude disguise should serve against casual observation. If the observation becomes less than casual, no disguise will serve," Chesterton concluded, his lined face breaking into a broad grin. "Hello!"

"What hello—"

"No, there!" Chesterton's voice held an urgency to it as George stared after Chesterton's outstretched arm. A column of tanks was rumbling over the far lip of low hills and into the valley. "Russians, George—let's ride for it." Chesterton's horse reared, wheeling.

George tugged at his animal's reins, bringing it around, shouting to Maradan, "Russians!"

There was a single gunshot. George felt his horse start to fall under him, its legs buckling. He threw himself clear, rolling, going for the .45 by his right kidney, the Colt Combat Government in his right fist as he looked up.

Turbans and women's headdresses were being thrown off, robes torn away. The caravan members were suddenly bristling with Soviet assault rifles. He looked to his right—helicopters closed from the direction from which he and the others had just come.

Behind him, Chesterton's mount stood motionless, the Browning Hi-Power in Chesterton's right hand. And behind Chesterton, from the far edge of the valley, more helicopters were closing in.

George looked to Maradan and the caravan leader—both men had their hands raised.

A tall man heavily built, bareheaded, wearing Soviet mountain fatigues partially revealed beneath an open gray robe, strode toward George.

In his right hand he casually held a pistol. "I am Colonel Dmitri Jurgenov. You and your compatriot," the Soviet officer announced in faultless English, "are under arrest. You have a choice. If you and the Englishman surrender, only Maradan and his men will be executed. Otherwise, the entire complement of the caravan, whom my men hold prisoner beyond the lines of tanks, will be shot." As if reading off a grocery list, Jurgenov continued. "Fourteen women, twenty-nine children, forty-two men. The choice is yours, Mr. Beegh."

George looked at the line of tanks. The Soviet colonel could be bluffing, but likely wasn't.

"This is your show, George—whatever you decide," he heard Sir Abner Chesterton say.

George rose to his full height—he was taller than the Russian, but not by much. "I'm going to shoot my horse and put him out of his misery, and then put my guns down. If you kill the hostages from the caravan, it won't do you any good that you've got us outnumbered. They won't be able to kill me fast enough to keep me from killing you."

The Soviet officer only smiled, then made a gesture of acquiescence with his weaponless left hand toward George's pistol and then toward the tortured horse.

George nodded, raised the .45 toward the animal and sighted on its head.

As he pulled the trigger and heard what sounded almost like a human scream, George Beegh closed his eyes....

GEORGE SAT ABOARD the Hind-A. Beside him sat the Soviet colonel. Three ships flew in formation, and in one of them was Sir Abner Chesterton. It had been hard watching Maradan die. But the Soviet colonel had not executed the hostages from the caravan.

After the firing squad had executed Maradan and his men, Colonel Jurgenov had turned to George and said, "I could have killed all of the hostages, just as easily. I do not spare their lives because of my promise to you. That is meaningless. I do not spare their lives from some fear of your reprisals—I can have you beaten senseless at my slightest whim. I spared the hostages for the simple reason that they have seen the might of Soviet power and they will tell others. And they will tell others that the Soviets can at once be cruel and merciful. For this reason only do they live. You live and the Englishman lives simply that I may fulfill my duty and return you alive to Alma Ata. What possible value your life may have, I have not felt the need to know."

Then he had turned on his heel and marched away.

George looked down now at his handcuffed hands. They looked no stronger than standard American police handcuffs, and if his life depended on doing so he felt that he could snap them.

His father and his mother were alive—he knew that now. And they were somehow important to the Soviet Union, important enough that he was wanted alive. He knew as well why Chesterton had not been killed. A friend could always be used as a wedge.

He tried to remember his mother's face beyond a fixed pose in a photograph.

He could remember her voice more.

And he remembered all the times she had cried.

Then his thoughts drifted to his father. His father had been the source of the tears.

If his father was the source of this, he wondered if he could kill his own blood.

He looked down below them, following the shadow of the stubby-winged helicopter over the cold desert. He wondered about Dan Track. His oldest friend, yet—George exhaled loudly, heavily.

Jurgenov spoke to him. "You may wonder at your destination. I am personally to deliver you and the Englishman to the Institute for Psycho-Physical Research outside Alma Ata, to Dr. Morton Tillman. He is a Canadian, and will at least speak your language. What he plans for you, I cannot say. But I understand—it is rumor only, mind you—that Dr. Tillman uses exotic drugs derived from certain plants to expand the power of the human mind to new boundaries. So perhaps some great adventure on the very limits of science awaits you, Mr. Beegh. But I also understand, and this is only rumor but rumor is sometimes so tantalizing, that these drugs eventually cause something far worse than any death I could have contrived for you. Again, something to look forward to, hmm?''

Jurgenov was smiling.

George forced himself to appear braver than he felt. He told the Soviet colonel, ''Let me confide in you—I think you're an asshole.''

Jurgenov looked away, shouting to the pilot, ''Use the radio. Tell Unit 2 that the Englishman is to be thrown from the machine to his death immediately.'' He spoke in English—George had noticed that all of the Soviet special forces personnel with Jurgenov spoke English well. He wondered why.

''Wait a minute—'' George began.

''You will threaten me again?''

''No, wait.''

''Wait? You chose to insult me. I should wait? You insult me, I kill your friend—it is as simple as that.''

''No—'' George could already hear the pilot relaying the order in English. ''I, ah, I apologize, all right?''

''Tell the pilot of Unit 2 to hang the Englishman from the side of the craft but not to let him fall—yet,'' Jurgenov said as he smiled. ''Your apology,'' he said, turning to face George, ''does not sound sincere.''

''It's sincere. Look, I really mean it.''

''Ah.'' Jurgenov nodded. ''If you are sincere, then you will doubtless wish to somehow demonstrate your sincerity.''

George licked his lips. His mouth had gone

suddenly dry as he saw Sir Abner Chesterton being put out onto the side of the machine. The door of the chopper closed, and Chesterton dangled from a sling. George looked at Jurgenov. "What do you want?"

"I shall have to consider what I would feel a sincere expression of your abject apology. After all, such a thing to say in front of my pilot, and the others here."

"What do you want me to do?" George asked quietly.

"I do believe you are getting the spirit of it. If I had a picture of your Statue of Liberty, perhaps I could make you urinate on it."

"Go to—" George clamped his lips shut, not finishing it.

"You are learning," Jurgenov said, laughing. "Instead, I'll choose something more personal. Stand up, I will release your seat belt," and he reached over, releasing the buckle. George tried to stand, but he was too tall, and had to bend his head. "Now, drop your pants—right now."

George looked at him. "And you'll bring sir Abner inside?" He glanced through the window, making sure sir Abner was still there, held by a piece of webbing around his waist.

"Yes, after a time. I have something else in mind."

"Someday I'll get you for this—that's a promise. If I have to come back from the grave to do it," George said, beginning to lose control.

"Drop your pants!" Jurgenov ordered.

George, his hands cuffed, undid his belt, popped the metal button at the belt line of his blue jeans, and pulled down his zipper. He pushed his pants down.

"Long underwear," Jurgenov commented. "Doubtless against the cold of the mountains. Push them down, Mr. Beegh, now or the Englishman falls to his death."

George looked at Jurgenov, saying nothing. He pushed down his underwear and stood bare from the waist to the ankles.

"You look very uncomfortable, Mr. Beegh. You like to speak of assholes. I see that you, like all of us, have one. The air outside this aircraft must be very cold indeed. I wish for you to repeat something until your voice is so strained you cannot speak, and then after that until your throat bleeds. Otherwise, the Englishman will be left on the outside of the aircraft for the duration of the flight and be quite dead."

"What—"

"And you will stand for the duration of the flight—only another two hours I should think until we make our next connection for Alma Ata. You will stand perfectly erect with your head bowed as it is beneath the roof of the machine. And you will repeat, 'I am an American asshole, and that is the biggest kind.' Otherwise, your English friend will suffer a worse death than the comparatively easy death of falling from the aircraft. He will gasp for breath in the cold air while his flesh withers and freezes and death comes very slowly. You may begin, and speak loudly enough that I may hear you above the noise of the rotors, please.''

"I am an—American asshole, and that is the biggest kind.''

"Louder.''

George shouted it.

"Louder.''

George screamed the words, his throat aching with it.

"Louder!''

He screamed his throat raw.

"Again. Do not stop or the Englishman will be returned to his perch.'' And Jurgenov laughed.

"I am an American asshole,'' George screamed, over and over and over. For the first time in his life he knew passionate hatred.

8

There was no knock, just a loud, crashing sound as the door of the farmhouse exploded inward. Two men in arctic clothing, their faces totally obscured, rushed inside, rifles in their hands, four more men came behind them.

Mariana Antonova saw her treasures—the little china pot, the cup and saucer, the plate—crash to the floor as one of the men smashed his rifle butt against the cabinet that held them. The cabinet toppled forward.

She screamed despite herself, and stood up from the rocking chair where she sat to face a gun pointed at her.

A seventh man entered the room. He wore a heavy overcoat and a broad-brimmed hat—a city hat.

"Who are you?" she asked, summoning the courage to speak.

"His car was outside—it must be his," the man said in a cold voice. "He has been here, but is not here now. We have watched through your windows. Where is he?"

"Who do you want?" she asked, but she knew it was Sergei.

She still held the note, and she knew enough about the workings of police to know that they would recognize his handwriting. "There was a traveler here. He spent the night out of the storm and he left."

"What did he tell you? Even the slightest detail could be of use to us."

She remembered Sergei Nicolai Baslovitch describing his troubles. "He said nothing. He was very surly. He drank my tea, he ate my bread and he slept the night and was gone by morning."

"Liar!" The man in the hat struck her across the face and she fell back against the hearth, her shawl falling from her head. She crumpled the note and thrust her hand into the fire to get the slip of paper so far back in the flames that the note would be irretrievable.

"Get her!" yelled one of the faceless men who had smashed down her door.

Her sleeve was on fire as rough hands dragged her from the hearth and threw her across the room. There was a shriek of pain as one of the men reached into the fire. "It is burned, Comrade Captain!"

The man in the hat wheeled to face her, straddling her. One of the soldiers with him handed him the half-empty bottle of vodka. He drank from it, then spit a mouthful of the vodka at her face. "You will tell me everything about this traveler, or you will surely die—and most slowly and unpleasantly."

She gasped the words. Her left hand clutched at her chest—it was on fire with pain. "I will die quickly—very quickly—"

The pain engulfed her and she surrendered to it as an act of will.

9

George could not speak, and did not wish to even if he had had the power. Chesterton sat beside him. They were in the passenger compartment of a business jet. Talking had been forbidden, but under his breath Chesterton hissed, "What happened back there?" George shook his head.

"I saw you spit up blood. What did they do to you?"

Again, George shook his head.

Jurgenov shouted back, "Silence—or perhaps the Englishman should dive from this aircraft, my young American friend." The Russian laughed.

George looked up from his manacled hands and stared at the back of Jurgenov's head, the crew-cut hair, blond and graying. In his mind he could see Jurgenov's deep-set brown eyes. Inside his head, George whispered words of hate. . . .

GEORGE STILL could not speak when he and Chesterton were shoved into the back of a small van and the doors locked, leaving them alone in total darkness.

Chesterton rasped, "What happened, George? Can you speak?"

George didn't bother to shake his head. Chesterton would not be able to see him anyway.

"If they threatened to kill me and you were forced to do something, well, my God, man, you are my friend and I would do the same for you. But not for me, please. I know they wanted to kill me, but then they didn't."

"It—it—my fault," George coughed, feeling the blood in his throat again and wanting to retch on it....

The van doors opened and George squinted against the light. He saw two civilians standing beyond the semicircle of fatigue-clad Soviet guards. One was his father. The other was his mother. George leaped from the rear of the van, guards grabbing at him. "Mom—mom!" But the woman looked through him, then smiled strangely for a moment and turned to the man. His mother said to his father, "Who is that boy, Morton?"

"Dad!" He screamed the word and his voice ached and the blood rose in his throat.

His father told his mother. "An American mercenary—quite insane. Captured in Afghanistan. We shall spare his life to aid in our research."

"It's me, George. Your son. Dad—mom! For God's sake?" A rifle butt hammered into his abdomen and he doubled forward and fell to his knees. Blood spewed from his mouth.

"If you say so, dear," he heard his mother say

calmly. And as he looked up, she was walking away.

George had it now. It was all an elaborate nightmare. He'd had nightmares about his parents ever since their death. He'd imagined all of this. He was in fever, delirious. Because this was the sort of insanity that occurred in nightmares but not in daylight in the real world.

He was staring down at the gravel where he'd fallen and he saw a pair of shoes. He looked up from them to his father's face. "You were right in calling her your mother, George. But she doesn't know she is your mother anymore. The drugs I've used have destroyed her, but they were necessary. But I'm not your father—I never was. Your father looked very much like me and I killed him because I wanted to kill him—but only after three years of using my drugs on his mind to drain all there was from it, about you, about your mother, about your heroic uncle. He was a stubborn man, your father. When I took his place, for reasons you'll come to know, I kept up the facade as best I could. But there was a natural handicap. I have never loved anyone. Now be a good son and let them lock you away until we begin."

George wept. His limits were being reached, quickly. The Russians were going to break him. "I'll kill you!" He said the words loudly, evenly.

George struggled to his feet.

"Oh, no you won't, George. Because I understand from Colonel Jurgenov's radio report that you hold deep feelings of friendship for the Englishman. And then, of course, there is your darling mother. I could release her from her misery very easily."

"When did my father die?"

"Let's see, you were born in 1959, wasn't it? We captured Robert Beegh at the lamasery where he studied the Tibetan techniques of the mind conquering the body—that was in 1961. Add three years and that makes it 1964 when I injected hydrochloric acid into his carotid artery. Rather a quick death." The man smiled. "Any other questions? Well, we'll take care of them later. You'll want to freshen up." With that the man turned away and said to the guards, "He is to be kept straitjacketed and there is to be a twenty-four-hour suicide watch! Take him!"

George felt their hands take hold of him roughly. He heard Chesterton saying, "Good God, man. I'm sorry—" And then a thudding sound and a groan. He looked behind him. Chesterton's body was limp, suspended under the armpits by two more of the guards.

"This may prove very interesting, it's a pity I must leave." Jurgenov laughed, turning away.

Under his breath, George swore he was going to get even.

10

There had been an ice storm in the evening, and now Dan Track could hear the tree branches above his head tinkling like a glass wind chime in the stiff cool breeze. But the sun was warm, and Track mentally bet that by midday most of the ice would be gone. It had taken longer than he had expected to reach the area outside Khorog. But now, in the distance, Track could see the Chinese house.

It was the perfect spot for a smuggler—near a main road and an airport. All morning, as Track had ridden beneath the tree cover, the sounds of various aircraft had disturbed the stillness. Yet, the house was remote, and was barely visible, nestled in the lowest of the foothills, its tiled roof hidden in the wooded area surrounding it.

Steam rose from the ground where the sunlight shone most brightly, giving the appearance of low-lying fog rolling in patches along the puddles of ice-crusted water. And steam escaped Track's horse's nostrils, as well as his own, as they exhaled.

He had evaded the Soviet patrol, avoiding an encounter at all costs—he had slightly less than three full magazines for the AK-47 and his supply of shot shells for the SPAS-12 was running low. Hakim Mohammed, his contact, was supposed to have the rest of Track's supplies, if all had gone as planned. And there was no reason, Dan Track reflected, to suppose that it had. Desiree had sent him by her most secure route from a place of non-Communist origin. Yet Soviet troops had been dogging his path. Rahman Mirza had been killed, along with all of his men. And Desiree had come herself; he'd soon see her at Mohammed's house. He wanted to see her, very badly, but did not want her inside the Soviet Union. And the most difficult part of his mission still lay ahead. He had to penetrate the Institute for Psycho-Physical Research near Alma Ata. Once inside, he had to find his sister, Diane, and his brother-in-law, Robert.

And then to play God, perhaps.

And then out of the Soviet Union again, with Diane in tow.

And if all of that could be done, what would he say to his nephew, George Beegh? "Look, son—I had to kill your dad because he was a Communist agent. But don't hold it against me, okay?" There would be nothing to say, nothing to do.

He'd had an idea, and it was taking hold. Even though he knew he would not last long in the Soviet Union, he felt he could make his presence felt.

As his horse broke from the trees, he could see a clear road leading to the house. Track reined the

Buz-Kashi horse back, and the animal reared slightly.

So far no security had been in evidence, and he wondered about the working arrangements that Hakim Mohammed had with the Soviet hierarchy of Khorog. Or did his connections extend all the way to Moscow?

The grounds were walled, but the wall looked like a very ordinary one, not something built for maximum security.

Track unlimbered the AK-47 and rested it across his thighs, then raised the SPAS-12 on its sling from beneath his right arm. He worked the action, chambering the first round from the magazine, checking the set of the safeties, then letting the police shotgun fall back to swing against his side.

He picked up the AK-47 and held the weapon by the pistol grip, his right index finger alongside the trigger guard, the buttstock pushed against his abdomen.

He gently nudged his heels against the flanks of his horse, urging the big animal forward.

There was still no sign of security as Track avoided the roadway, keeping the horse to the ice-crusted early-winter grass.

As he approached to within two hundred yards, Track could detect movement at the gate set in the wall surrounding the house. He worked the bolt of the AK-47, stripping the top round from the magazine, chambering it. He checked to see that the selector was properly set, to auto.

When he was about a hundred yards away, the gates began to swing open and he could make out the form of a garden and courtyard beyond them.

Then a figure walked from the open gates, the figure tall but slight, with a massive fur hat all but obscuring the head.

And then the hat was pulled away, and a mane of black hair cascaded around the face. The figure started running toward him. Dan Track dug in his heels and the horse sprang ahead. Track's right thumb worked the safety tumbler of the AK-47, and he clutched the rifle like a high-wire walker's balance pole as he aimed the horse toward the running woman.

Track skidded his horse to a halt and slid from the saddle, letting the AK-47 slip from his fingers to the ice-crusted grass as he ran the few remaining yards. Then he swept Desiree into his arms, his mouth pushing down on hers, her fingertips caressing his face....

TRACK FELT THE HEAT of Desiree's body beneath the sheet that covered their bed in Hakim Mohammed's house. Earlier, Track had showered until his skin had tingled with the hot water, eaten, and consumed several glasses of a blended whiskey. All the while, they had talked, Track recounting the events since leaving her base inside Pakistan.

Desiree snuggled close beside him; the room temperature was cool, good for lovemaking. "I've been doing some thinking,'' Track said softly. "After this, can you get Diane out without me?"

Her body stiffened slightly against him, and Desiree whispered close to his face, her breath warm against his cheek. "You're going to make the Russians pay for this business with your sister, aren't you?"

"Have you added mind reading to your abilities?" he said, realizing after he said it that the words sounded very cold.

She sat up beside him, tucking the sheet around her body under her arms, covering her breasts with it. "Aren't you?" she repeated.

"Yeah, I think I have to," he told her as he rolled over on his side, not looking at her.

"You know you won't come back," she said. "The Russians won't make the same mistake twice. I'll probably never see you again."

He exhaled heavily. "If I do make it out I'll head straight for you. Where else would I go?"

"Why are you doing this?" he heard her ask, her voice lifeless.

"It sounds stupid," he replied. "But I figure maybe I have a better chance of doing it than anyone else does. I guess somebody has to show those Soviet shits they can't sit tucked back nice and safe and play their goddamn evil games without somebody paying them back. It looks like that someone is me."

"You could start a war—and not the kind that would be good for my business, either."

"No, if I make it at all, the U.S. government will deny they ever heard of me—at least they'll try to. And you know me, I'm not kill happy. I never have been. I'm not going to go breaking into the Kremlin and assassinate somebody. That's not my way. But if I can break up some of their operations inside the Soviet Union, maybe get some of the resistance people who work underground to go after something that will really hurt—I don't know." Track felt Desiree's warm hands against his bare shoulders, and continued to think aloud. "If the Soviet leaders start realizing that operations inside Russia can be hit, maybe they'll start turning their attention inward and it'll make it that much easier on the rest of the world. Things might be a hell of a lot better if they didn't feel so damn safe. Maybe I can make them feel afraid, even just a little."

"Then I'll help you," Desiree said decisively. "I have contacts in Soviet underground. I can still smuggle anything I want into the Soviet Union."

"Or out?"

"Not as easy. The border is designed more to keep people in, the reverse of what it would be in a Western nation. That's why Hakim Mohammed is so successful here—smuggling things into Soviet territory isn't as difficult as it might seem. There are more guards, but that just means more people who can be bribed to look the other way. And since consumer goods are so high priced and so hard to get, you can work miracles with something like a wristwatch."

"Who loves you most?" Track asked her, looking over his shoulder at Desiree, smiling, "Rolex or Timex."

Desiree Goth laughed. "It depends on how important what I'm smuggling happens to be." Track still watched her, her smile going, her eyes pinpoints of light beneath her lashes. "Of course," she continued, "I could give all this up. We could go away together. I have more money than we could spend in a dozen lifetimes."

"Was that a proposal?" And he turned toward her, folding her into his arms as the sheet across her breasts fell away. He could feel the heat of her body.

"Yes," she replied, looking into his eyes.

"Then I accept—but we'll have to wait a while."

"Then you're going through with this?"

"Yes, I have to," Track whispered, his lips beside her right ear. The diamond in her earlobe caught the light for an instant, and broke it like a prism.

"Then I'll help you. My contacts in the Soviet Union are mostly Jewish, fighting repression. I can smuggle in the equipment you'll need—guns, ammunition, electronic surveillance toys—if it will help to get you out again and back to me."

Very quietly, holding her face in his hands, he told her, "All right, then." And he kissed her, holding her for a very long time. And after that, he slipped between her thighs and she whispered things to him that he had never known. It made what he would do at once harder and easier. But mostly harder.

11

Hakim Mohammed, a squat-looking man with
dark heavy features and incongruous green eyes,
had joined them in the range located two floors underground beneath his house. Mohammed had
been away on his business when Track had arrived,
and now he had unceremoniously joined them as
Track began unlimbering the weapons Desiree had
smuggled across the Sino-Soviet border for him.

"I will pay you a thousand of your dollars for
that revolver, Major Track," were the first words
Hakim Mohammed offered.

Dan Track looked at the four-inch Metalife Custom L-Frame stainless Smith & Wesson, and then
at the green eyes of Hakim Mohammed. "But it
wouldn't do you any good, it has my name on the
right barrel flat," he replied.

"I can have the engraving buffed away and my
own name placed there."

"I appreciate the compliment, but the revolver is
very much a part of me." Track set the L-Frame
.357 on the table beside the sample case and
reached inside the case again, withdrawing a Trapper Scorpion .45. "This one isn't for sale, either."

"A pity. It appears handmade."

"It is." Track grinned. "It goes with the L-Frame—too much a part of me to sell." Desiree had insisted that Track avoid using his own weapons when crossing from Pakistan into Afghanistan, in the event a gun should be lost and betray his presence there. He had agreed, but now there was no point in denying himself the use of his personalized guns—the Russians were expecting him.

He set the Trapper .45 down beside the Metalife Custom L-Frame.

Desiree began what sounded like a litany as he began unpacking the rest of the case. "Two Walther P-5s fitted with silencers—I had the silencers custom-made and they are very good. Both of the Walthers are fitted with slide locks if you should need them extra quiet. And I can provide you with subsonic ammunition if need be."

"All right," Track answered, affixing the silencer to one of the Walthers and taking the heft of the pistol. It balanced well.

As if reading his mind, Desiree said, "The butt of the pistol has been internally altered to add about an extra six ounces of weight so with the silencer attached it doesn't feel muzzle heavy."

Track set the pistol down, and Desiree continued—the arms salesman to the end. "This is a Randall .45, a service model, virtually identical to the Colt but in stainless steel. The rear sight is higher-profiled and the grip safety is a modified beavertail. It has a long trigger—I thought you might prefer it that way."

Track nodded as he took a second stainless-steel .45 from the case, identical to the first.

"A spare," Desiree told him simply. He took a revolver from the case, an L-Frame like his own but with a fixed rear sight, standard factory service stocks and apparently no custom work. "I thought a standard .357 with nothing done to it might prove useful under some circumstances. This is a very good one. It should shoot almost as well as your custom gun."

Track swung open the cylinder, checking that it was empty, then gave the cylinder a spin, watching for wobble of the ejector rod—there was none. He closed the cylinder—the space above and below was even. Holding the revolver beside his right ear, he slowly thumbcocked the hammer, the fingers of his left hand tensioning against the cylinder to feel for lockup. It was perfect. He lowered the hammer. "This is a good one."

Desiree smiled, a professional smile that made Track laugh.

"If you'll follow me to the larger case by the far wall," she began, then laughed. "I'm sorry—force of habit."

"That's all right," Track told her.

As they walked, she continued talking, the clicking of her high heels punctuating her words. "On the Randall .45s, if you remove the left grip panel you'll notice the frames have been drilled and tapped for use with the Clark Aimpoint sight mounts. I've provided two of these and a supply of batteries to operate the sights. I can resupply you with those as necessary." She crouched beside a box the size of a small coffin, and pushed the lid back. As she stood, she said, "Three more SPAS-12s—that gives you four of them. Four AKMs. If I had got you AKS-74s, ammunition resupply for you inside the Soviet Union might have been difficult—they're not in wide circulation yet. Four Walther MPK submachine guns, all four of them fitted for silencers—I have those packed separately."

"You knew, didn't you," Track said to her.

"I suspected. Don't forget, Dan, I know you very well."

"One man isn't going to need all of this—" he began.

"I anticipated that," she said with a grin and continued to run down the arsenal. "Two Steyr-Mannlicher Special Rifles, the SSGs. Both 7.62mm NATO."

"What do you mean, you anticipated this?" Track asked her pointedly.

Desiree's response was to look past Track and say, "Ah, here he is." Track turned to follow her gaze. Stepping from the elevator and into the range was the giant figure he had known for as long as he had known Desiree. The neon lights on the ceiling reflected from the hairless head, and the eyes beneath the heavy eyebrows were at once laughing and remote.

The man extended his dark brown hand. "Major," he said.

"Zulu," Track replied, taking Zulu's hand.

"It appears we shall be working closely together."

"Now wait a minute," Track began, releasing Zulu's hand, looking at Desiree.

"I have already discussed this with Zulu," she said. "He too has a score to settle with the Communists—Russia backed the Communist revolutionaries in the Congo who killed his wife and family. Besides, even you can't do this alone."

Track let out a long sigh, listening as Desiree said, "You couldn't ask for a better man, and because Zulu so loves me, he'll bring you home to me—whenever that will be."

Track looked at Zulu. "You really want to do this?"

"Miss Desiree asked my sentiments, Major. Naturally, I had some trepidations. Leaving Miss Desiree's affairs unattended to, her own personal security and the like. But I shall assist you in this matter regarding your sister. It is an affair of honor that needs resolution and I would be pleased to aid you in making what was wrong right."

"Two are better than one, Dan. And no one will fight like Zulu, or think like him," Desiree whispered.

Hakim Mohammed spoke. "Then I assumed correctly—this man—" he gestured to Dan Track

"—intends to penetrate Soviet territory to carry out some sort of commando operation?"

"Yes," Desiree said quietly.

"If the Soviets learn of my involvement in this, however peripheral, my business associations could be ruined."

Desiree, her voice firm, told him, "Without my smuggling contacts you would have no business. Without those things that I supply you, your associates would soon tire of your services and you would be imprisoned. Without me, you are nothing. You have served me faithfully in the past, and I have no doubt that you shall continue to serve me." She stepped between Track and Zulu. "I have always found that your pledge," she said to Mohammed, "was all the contract I needed, something I could rely upon in all matters. I ask that pledge from you now. What transpires here must remain secret, and you will aid Major Track and Zulu as you would serve me."

Hakim Mohammed licked his lips. Dan Track thought if there could be a female Godfather, Desiree could qualify. And then Hakim Mohammed bowed slightly to her, saying, "I will not disappoint you, Desiree." Desiree stepped forward, planting a kiss on Hakim Mohammed's right cheek. "Never," the Arab reiterated.

SUNLIGHT FILTERED THROUGH the curtains and across the low red table before the couch. Track sat forward, listening as the soft-spoken Hakim Mohammed's voice emanated from the heavy jowls surrounding his rather small mouth. "My contacts tell me that the institute of which you speak has always been heavily guarded, but within the past ten days the guard has been increased."

Desiree, kneeling on the floor at Track's feet, her legs tucked under her, her right arm draped across Track's knees, puffed on a cigarette, exhaling a cloud of smoke with a loud, dramatic hiss. "Major Track and Zulu must get inside," she said. "You will tell me how."

Zulu, sitting at the opposite end of the couch from Track, his Oxford-accented baritone very low, added, "And, of course, how we may afterward extricate ourselves. That, too, might prove useful, Mr. Mohammed."

"Yes, but it will be very difficult. If I understand correctly, the major and Zulu intend to penetrate the institute, then forcibly if necessary remove the director of the institute and his wife."

"Yes," Track agreed, studying the tip of his cigar. "You've got it."

"Then perhaps I should mention an incidental piece of intelligence that I was fortunate enough to acquire on my recent excursion to Alma Ata on Desiree's behalf."

"That is why he was not here when you arrived, Dan," Desiree added absently.

"Yes," Hakim Mohammed said, standing, his flabby body jiggling as he began to pace the room.

Unlike most Moslems—or at least the religious ones—Mohammed drank, and he carried a small glass of bourbon in his left hand. "Within the past few days, two persons have been brought to the institute. This in itself is not uncommon—it is said that the Russians experiment there on human beings."

"What sort of experiments?" Zulu asked suddenly.

"What people?" Track interrupted.

"To answer Zulu first. It is rumored to be mind control—but using the human mind beyond its ordinary capabilities. As weapons."

"What people?" Track said again.

"Westerners. A group of Soviet special forces personnel delivered them. Their leader was a Colonel Dmitri Jurgenov, an exceptionally brilliant, exceptionally bestial man."

"Who were the people?" Track insisted.

"A man in his fifties, very trim, gray hair, above average height."

"Sir Abner Chesterton," Track said soullessly.

"And with this Englishman," Hakim Mohammed began again, "there was a young man—very tall, unshaven, his hair almost black. There was an instance where he came in some conflict with the special forces personnel and flung one of them some two meters away from him. But then a pistol was placed against the head of the Englishman and the younger man raised his hands."

"George." It was Desiree who said it.

"Shit," Track shouted, slamming his fist on the table.

"Oh, well put, Major," Zulu said as he applauded. . . .

THEY STILL SAT in the living room of Hakim Mohammed's house. A woman servant, old and frail, had brought drinks for Desiree, Zulu and Track. Mohammed had stopped his pacing and had sagged heavily into an overstuffed chair opposite the couch.

Zulu suddenly stood. "Here, Major—here is why my aid in this expedition will be of the most inestimable value. I can view our task with greater detachment." And Zulu, his hands thrust deep into the pockets of his tailored brown tweed slacks, began to pace. "It is regrettable, of course, that Sir Abner and your young nephew appear to have fallen into enemy hands. Yet, it is dubious that George would suffer injury at the hands of his mother and father. So we can assume that for the time being George is to a degree safe. And likewise, I think, Sir Abner Chesterton. If some sort of acquiescence is sought from George to his father's work on behalf of the Soviet Union, then the execution or permanent maiming of Sir Abner would be counterproductive. Would you not agree?"

His eyes wide, his broad bony face more animated than Track had ever seen it, Zulu seemed waiting for a response. Track gave him one. "Yeah, maybe."

"Excellent. Then follow my reasoning. If we can feel justified in assuming their well-being, then their very incarceration may prove an advantage."

"Bullshit—I took Logic 101 too, okay. George's dad turned, maybe—or maybe something else. But from what Mr. Mohammed said—"

"Please, Major, I am called by my friends Hakim."

Track nodded, trying to pick up his train of thought. "But from what Hakim told us, it sounds like they were getting rough treatment."

"Quite," Zulu agreed. "But, not fatal treatment. There is the key. With George and Sir Abner inside the installation, we have two potential allies whom we can arm to aid in our escape. And possibly be at least equally efficacious in aiding our entry."

"You lost me," Track admitted.

"He is saying," Hakim Mohammed began, "that if word somehow could be got to them inside the institute—"

"Exactly," Zulu said, smiling. "We should assume George is under the closest of scrutiny. Yet, Sir Abner Chesterton may well be in some holding area, as a bargaining chip against George's actions. If a man could reach Chesterton with a pistol and perhaps some plastique—"

"That is out of the question," Hakim Mohammed interrupted.

"How much would it cost?" Desiree asked him calmly.

HE'S EXPLOSIVE. HE'S MACK BOLAN... AGAINST ALL ODDS

He learned his deadly skills in Vietnam...then put them to good use by destroying the Mafia in a blazing one-man war. Now **Mack Bolan** ventures further into the cold to take on his deadliest challenge yet—the KGB's worldwide terror machine.

Follow the lone warrior on his exciting new missions...and get ready for more nonstop action from his high-powered combat teams: **Able Team**—Bolan's famous Death Squad—battling urban savagery too brutal and volatile for regular law enforcement. And **Phoenix Force**—five extraordinary warriors handpicked by Bolan to fight the dirtiest of antiterrorist wars, blazing into even greater danger.

Fight alongside these three courageous forces for freedom in all-new action-packed novels! Travel to the gloomy depths of the cold Atlantic, the scorching sands of the Sahara, and the desolate Russian plains. You'll feel the pressure and excitement building page after page, with nonstop action that keeps you enthralled until the explosive conclusion!

Now you can have all the new Gold Eagle novels delivered right to your home!

You won't want to miss a single one of these exciting new action-adventures. And you don't have to! Just fill out and mail the card at right, and we'll enter your name in the Gold Eagle home subscription plan. You'll then receive six brand-new action-packed Gold Eagle books every other month, delivered right to your home! You'll get two Mack Bolan novels, one Able Team and one Phoenix Force, plus one book each from two thrilling, new Gold Eagle libraries, **SOBs** and **Track**. In **SOBs** you'll meet the legendary team of mercenary warriors who fight for justice and win. **Track** features a military and weapons genius on a mission to stop a maniac whose dream is everybody's worst nightmare. Only Track stands between us and nuclear hell!

FREE! The New War Book and Mack Bolan bumper sticker.

As soon as we receive your card we'll rush you the long-awaited New War Book and Mack Bolan bumper sticker—both ABSOLUTELY FREE with your first six Gold Eagle novels.

The New War Book is *packed* with exciting information for Bolan fans: a revealing look at the hero's life...two new short stories...book character biographies...even a combat catalog describing weapons used in the novels! The New War Book is a special collector's item you'll want to read again and again. And it's yours FREE when you mail your card!

Of course, you're under no obligation to buy anything. Your first six books come on a 10-day free trial—if you're not thrilled with them, just return them and owe nothing. The New War Book and bumper sticker are yours to keep, FREE!

Don't miss a single one of these thrilling novels...mail the card now, while you're thinking about it.

"I do not—" Mohammed gan.

"How much will it cos Desiree asked again, her voice firm.

"There is one guar   —"

"How much, H im?" Desiree asked again.

"He would ne to change his identity, to begin a new life, to—'

Desiree s od, her hands moving to her hips, her voice rais g. "How much?" she shouted.

"Th equivalent of a hundred thousand dollars— in gold."

When do you need it?" Desiree asked.

"I have it here, but—" Hakim Mohammed be-an.

"I will replace it for you, and double it for your help," Desiree said.

"No," Track said, reaching up and grabbing at her right forearm. She looked back at him once.

Hakim Mohammed looked at the two of them and shrugged. "I shall forgo profit," he said. "The one hundred thousand dollars alone will suffice." Then he stood, and gave her a little bow.

12

Sir Abner Chesterton sat in darkness. He was not terribly uncomfortable. He had been allowed to bathe when he'd first arrived, and had bathed once since. A small toilet was on the far side of the room and he had learned the layout of the cell well enough that he could find his way around in the total darkness. He was fed two meals a day. One, presumably breakfast, consisted of a cup of water and two crusts of bread. The other, dinner, was usually tepid, thin soup, more bread and something that was, he imagined, tea. During the meals, ten minutes as he gauged it, a bulb on the ceiling of his cell was lit. After each meal, the bulb was removed and he was plunged into darkness.

Intentionally, he would sometimes not eat the food. They were conditioning a reflex into him and he knew that and fought against it.

But it was neither breakfast nor dinner now, and a light suddenly flooded his cell. He squinted against the overpowering brightness, standing up from the floor where he'd been sitting on his folded blanket. The blanket, the toilet and the clothes on his back were all that was in the room.

His mouth was dry.

"You will come," a voice said in broken English.

"Certainly—my pleasure, I think," and Chesterton started for the door, looking forward to the prospect of movement beyond his cell.

A cloth bag was brought forward, then pushed down over his head. As anonymous hands secured the bag around his neck, he could feel the rough material of the bag scratch against his skin. The bag smelled of sweat and fear.

Hands gripped his upper arms and propelled him forward. His legs were stiff from his confinement, and he stumbled frequently. He counted his steps, trying to gauge distances. Suddenly, there was the sound of a pneumatic hiss and a door opening, closing. Suddenly, his body was racked with cold and he shivered and lost his footing, starting to go down. But the hands on his upper arms held him and he felt a knee slam against his rear end and he kept moving. Three men, he supposed.

"Might I ask where—"

"Silence!"

These were not the special forces troops, he decided. For one thing, their English was atrocious. He had tried striking up conversations with his feeder, but the man had rarely spoken a word.

If he could just find a weapon. Suddenly the heat was stifling and a door slammed shut behind him. He was marched on, another right turn and then he was stopped.

He heard one of his guards knock on a metal

door. The door opened and he was propelled forward.

Then the movement stopped and his hands were drawn behind him and he felt handcuffs being applied. The hood remained in place.

He stood completely still.

"Mr. Chesterton," a voice said, "you are standing on a rubber pad at the center of a large room." Chesterton recognized Morton Tillman's voice. "The floor is charged with electricity—ten thousand volts," Tillman continued. "The rubber pad that insulates you from it is specially designed to protect you. But it is very expensive to make. So it is only eighteen inches by eighteen inches. After a time, your legs will lose their feeling and your balance will go off, you may fall, or step off the pad. If so, you will surely die. I sit here, relaxing, sipping coffee. Later perhaps, I'll have a glass of sherry. Then later, dinner will be brought to me. Later still, I'll read a book. I so enjoy your British novelists."

"What do you want?" Chesterton interrupted, his legs feeling unsteady.

"Nothing, really. You see, George is watching this on closed-circuit television. Your fate is not in your hands, but in George's hands, I'm afraid."

"George! Whatever it is, don't do it, George!" Chesterton shouted.

"Such bravado," Tillman murmured. "But George cannot hear you. His head is locked into a vise so he cannot turn away. His eyelids have been taped open so he cannot close out the vision. He has been asked a simple request, really—"

"To kill you, I hope," Chesterton snapped.

The room around him filled with laughter. "No, no one would have to request that. I have found guilt to be even stronger than hatred. George's hands are secure behind him. Actually, the vise in which his head is locked has one free area. Beneath his chin. It is the only way he could avoid watching your eventual death—to move his head down. But he is secured to a laboratory table, lying on his stomach. By now I imagine his neck must be feeling as stiff as your legs feel weak. I have learned that both guilt and helplessness break the will. This experiment will achieve one or the other. Guilt if his head sags and depresses the switch located beneath his chin—in which case he will flood his mother's cell with poison gas and she will die very painfully. He can see her on another monitor. If he kills her, you will go free. He thinks. If he keeps his head up, you will eventually succumb to exhaustion and fall to the floor and be electrocuted. His third option is to surrender his will to me. To voluntarily submit to my drug therapy."

There was silence. Then, Sir Abner Chesterton cleared his throat. "I hope, Tillman, that when you die, you discover that there truly is a heaven. And that you find your soul among those forever excluded from it. You bastard."

Tillman's laughter was his only response.

GEORGE BEEGH SUCKED IN HIS BREATH against the pain in his neck and eyes. His head throbbed. His arms were drawn tightly behind him, his legs drawn up and shackled at the ankles to his wrists, his back bent against itself. He wanted to scream with the pain. But he could not—the heavy adhesive tape was bound over his mouth and made him want to retch.

He held his head up, his eyes streaming tears from being taped open. But he could see, just as Morton Tillman had planned it. He was being forced to stare at two television monitors. On one, a hooded and handcuffed Sir Abner Chesterton stood on a small rubber mat in a large room. On the second monitor, his mother lay on a bed, her face peaceful in sleep. Above her head dangled a hose. Tillman had told him that the hose was connected to a canister of nerve gas. The gas would kill his mother, but slowly, the muscle spasms awakening her from sleep as she fought for breath.

Tillman had given him a choice, his mother's life or the life of a man he had come to think of as a good friend. He wondered about his uncle. Had Dan Track betrayed him, somehow starting all of this by opening the old wound of Diane Beegh's death?

For the first time in a long time his loyalties were confused.

Taped into George's left hand was a small device with an electronic signal button. He could push that button, and neither Chesterton nor his mother would die. But the price would be his willing submission to Tillman's mind-control drugs.

What was the point of fighting, he thought. If they had so easily captured him and Chesterton, perhaps they had already caught Track. There would be no one to save him, no reason to stall and risk possible death for his mother or for Sir Abner Chesterton.

George wanted to close his eyes—it would let him think more clearly.

Instead, he pressed the button, admitted defeat, resigned his will to the man he so wished to kill.

13

Once, while waiting to murder a man who had originally been a Soviet agent, then become a double for the British, Sergei Baslovitch had been forced to sit through a very boring seminar about fire insurance. Later, after killing the traitor—he was a traitor to nearly everyone, having run off on his wife to take up with a younger woman, then cheating on the younger woman with a homosexual lover—Baslovitch had reflected on the central theme of the seminar. Insurance is always a luxury until you need it.

His own insurance had been a dear luxury, but now he needed it.

Omsk was a nice town, and it had only taken two more stolen cars to get there. Until the late nineteenth century, the town had been the headquarters of the fierce Siberian Cossacks. Now it was the headquarters for leather-goods and synthetic-rubber manufacturers.

The warehouse complex he now surveyed was guarded by standard security. The buildings themselves housed farm machinery, textiles, automobile and truck tires and the like.

But one of them housed something very special.

Business hours were still in effect and Baslovitch presented himself to the manager of the warehouse complex as Captain Vassily Kerenski. It was the name the manager had always known him by.

They exchanged pleasantries and knowing winks and with the inevitable desire of a lower echelon civilian to be privy to a closely guarded government secret, the warehouse manager had assured him the special operations base was quite safe.

Baslovitch told the man that his name was highly regarded for discretion in certain very important circles on Derzhinsky Square.

The manager then gave Baslovitch a nod and offered to walk back with him.

Baslovitch replied that it was unnecessary, adding that it would be best to alert the night watchman that there might well be important activity tonight.

Baslovitch had then left the small wooden office and walked toward the rear of the complex.

He stopped before the last building. The padlock was still in place and Baslovitch used his key to open it. Stepping inside, he used the interior padlock to secure the door.

The warehouse smelled of dust, and only one of the three overhead fixtures still possessed a working bulb. Baslovitch did not need light, knowing the warehouse like the back of his hand.

He stopped at the far wall, turned on his heel and paced off six meters. He took a folding knife from his pocket and inserted the point of the blade between two boards. Easily, he raised the board to the right. Closing the knife, he raised the board on the left, exposing a flat section of wooden sub-floor with a metal ring in it. He tugged at the metal ring, and the floorboard came up on its hinges.

Taking a small flashlight from his trench coat pocket, Baslovitch started down the set of stairs the light revealed.

At the base of the stairs, he shone the flashlight up, picking out the cord for a ceiling fixture. A spiderweb was attached to it. He swatted the spiderweb away with his gloved left hand, tugging on the cord. The bulb burned, and as he switched off the flashlight, he looked around the basement.

Everything was as he had left it.

The sealed containers of food, the ammunition, the clothing, whiskey, even the hot plate—everything was as it should be.

He plugged in the hot plate to the wall outlet and went to the nearest of the airtight plastic containers, opening the latch and then the hermetic seal. He could smell the aroma of the coffee packed along with food of various types inside. This was his insurance.

THERE HAD BEEN no opportunity for a shower, but using some of the stored water Baslovitch had managed to scrub his body and wash his hair. He sat now, in his secure safe house in the middle of those who were now his enemies, reveling in the clean clothes he wore and the dry shoes that covered his feet.

His belly was full, and the whiskey he now drank lit a fire inside him.

Leaning beside his chair was an AKM, and beside it on the floor, near the toe of the buttstock, two full magazines.

A moment of peace, he thought.

He wondered what the dream of 1917 had become. What had the Revolution freed his people from?

Baslovitch put down his whiskey and stood, a little shakily. He was tired, but there was no time to sleep.

A kettle whistled on the hot plate; he would need to get some coffee inside him.

He poured the boiling water into his cup and waited a moment for the instant coffee to settle, then he stirred it and took a sip. It tasted as if dirty socks had been boiled in it.

He shook his head to clear it.

In the container with the extra clothing was the uniform of a Soviet air force captain.

He figured he could live with the single grade reduction, and he began to strip away the comfortable clothes he had put on after his improvised shower, replacing them with the air force uniform.

He thought about Tatiana—he did not even

have her picture, and if he had, he would have destroyed it. Lest he be caught and she be questioned and sent away someplace very cruel.

Sergei Baslovitch continued to wonder what the Revolution of 1917 had indeed become, and inside him it sickened him that he thought that he knew. . . .

BASLOVITCH HAD DONE POORLY in forgery at the Chicago espionage school, and when he had prepared his little hideaway and realized the necessity of false papers and other identity documents he had made the acquaintance of a very pretty young woman who was expert at it. Updating the papers now in his basement safe house, Baslovitch hoped she had taught him well.

He had decided to forgo the AKM in favor of an Uzi submachine gun that nestled snugly in a leather attaché case, something he'd picked up in the United States.

A Walther P-38 rested in the bottom of his stuff sack, and beneath his uniform jacket was a Heckler & Koch P-7 9mm. In the outer right pocket of his greatcoat was a second P-7.

All of these would do him little good if he was discovered, but he had taken steps to remedy that as well, coloring his hair with Fanci-Full hair coloring, shade number 56—Bashful Blond, to match the photos on the identity cards. Now he'd see if blonds really do have more fun, he thought.

THE NIGHT WATCHMAN had been very respectful but very inquisitive as Baslovitch—now Captain André Goroschikov—had left the warehouse complex. "How did you get in, Comrade?" the man asked.

"I shall forget you asked that. You should have been more vigilant," Baslovitch said as he walked quickly away.

Another stolen car—Baslovitch smiled at that. If worst came to worst if and when he did reach the West, he could at least support himself in good style. He drove the car now toward the civilian airport outside Omsk, the headlights burning a hole in the darkness ahead of him.

Thinking of Tatiana only depressed him, and he thought instead of the things he had considered before changing into the air force uniform, scratching absently at the fake blond mustache he had applied to his upper lip. He hoped the glue held.

He drove on, getting closer to the airfield. It was not a military base, but like anything involving transportation inside the Soviet Union, especially long-distance transport, it was guarded. As the airport came in sight, he slowed the car. It would be necessary to get past the two guards at the gate one way or the other. All he needed was to steal a plane that was fueled. No big deal. He could already see several likely candidates, and among these his choice was one of the Antonov

AN-2Ms that dotted the edges of the field. The M-models were agricultural aircraft, less likely to be missed since they, like agriculture, were largely out of season with the coming cold. Besides, he was carrying a set of master keys for an Antonov that he had squirreled away in his safe house.

Baslovitch stopped the car, leaving the engine running—starting it had been difficult and he had no key. He exited the car, not wanting the guards at the gate to notice the absence of an ignition key.

As a corporal and a private started to approach him, Baslovitch automatically went for his papers.

"Comrade Captain," the corporal said as he saluted. "May I see your papers, please."

"Certainly," and he withdrew his left hand from his pocket and presented the papers. "A cold evening," Baslovitch remarked, rubbing both hands together before stuffing them back into the pockets of his open greatcoat.

"Very cold, Comrade Captain." A flashlight was flicked on for the inspection of the papers. "It is most late, Comrade Captain, to inspect the logs of the control tower supervisor," the corporal said.

"You are quite perceptive, Corporal, and so it is the best time."

There was the flicker of a smile on the corporal's face, and he handed back the papers. The flashlight clicked off and the corporal rendered a salute. "A pleasant evening to you, Comrade Captain."

Baslovitch returned the salute. "And to you, Corporal," he added as he placed the papers back in his pocket and started for the car. The forgery techniques the young woman had taught him had apparently been good enough.

He was opening the car door when he heard the voice behind him and froze. "A moment, Captain."

Baslovitch turned, neither smiling nor frowning, and stared back toward the two guards. "Yes?"

"The controller, Comrade Captain, will have less warning of your inspection if you drive to the far end of the control building."

Baslovitch wanted to let out a long breath. Instead, he nodded, tossing "Thank you, Comrade," into the night and turning back toward his car.

As he sat behind the wheel, he realized his palms were sweaty inside his gloves.

The engine sputtered—he willed it not to die. The guards would come to help and discover the automobile was hot-wired. That would be a tough one to explain. He did not want to kill them.

But the engine clung to life, he let out the clutch and the car moved forward. The corporal gave a salute, and Baslovitch nodded and drove on. He would park the vehicle behind the terminal control building as advised....

THE RURAL AIRFIELD was deserted at this late hour, and Baslovitch left the car where it would seem least conspicuous.

Rather than entering the control building, he walked toward the far edge of the field, keeping close to the shadows, heading toward one of the Antonov biwings. There was no reason to assume it would be fully fueled, but he could taxi the plane nearer another aircraft and siphon, or utilize his false identity papers again and have gasoline pumped for it.

He kept moving, his palms sweating inside his gloves more than they had sweated since the days of his first mission outside Soviet territory. There was no movement on the field.

Baslovitch kept walking, the nearer of the three Antonov single engine AN-2Ms looming out of the shadows cast by the airfield lighting.

He stopped less than a dozen yards from the aircraft, scanning right and left. He spotted no one. His luck was so phenomenally good that it worried him. The planes would be empty of gasoline and the pumps would be dry, he thought, smiling at the grisly prospect.

He wanted an Antonov for two reasons. He could fly it low enough to avoid radar detection and the sight of such a common plane—more than ten thousand had been produced in the Soviet Union and in Poland since 1947—would arouse little suspicion.

Baslovitch reached into the interior pocket of his greatcoat and fished out a bulky set of keys. Setting down his attaché case, Baslovitch glanced over his shoulder to confirm that he was not observed and began playing with the master keys.

One minute and a dozen keys later, he found the right one and slipped it from the ring. Pulling open the door, he let himself inside and climbed behind the controls. The plane was cold. He began fiddling with the set of keys again, looking for one that would fit the ignition. The third key he tried slipped effortlessly into the lock and the ignition switch turned freely. Removing the key from the ring he replaced it in the switch and turned the switch to the battery position. The gauges quickly showed life.

The fuel gauge registered full.

He glanced behind him into the fuselage storage compartment—gasoline containers. Baslovitch slid from behind the yoke and lifted a few. The containers were of the right weight to be full. He opened one and sniffed it—gasoline.

Entering from the fuselage door, he had passed several sacks of something he assumed to be fertilizer. But now after inspecting the gas canisters, he dropped to one knee before passing them again. Out came the big Puma lock-blade knife, and he cut through the outer canvas covering of one of the bags. Beneath it was a layer of cloth, and beneath that was plastic. He cut through the plastic, and right away he knew why the aircraft was fueled and ready.

Marijuana.

Drugs were as popular in the East as they were

in the West, and because of the tighter restrictions on individual activity and the somewhat greater degree of difficulty in illegal pursuits, the price was all that the traffic would bear and then more.

Baslovitch sighed and started forward again into the cockpit, settling himself behind the yoke. Of all the planes to choose, this one was the worst. Somebody was bound to notice its absence, and soon.

He gunned the single 1000 HP radial engine to life, and the aircraft was suddenly vibrating around him. The hum of the engine, the steadiness of its beat were reassuring.

He watched the oil pressure and engine temperature gauges register at operating level, and adjusted the leaning of the mixture—it would be colder flying at night.

He estimated that in another few minutes he would be airborne, on his way to Alma Ata, and there to intercept Track at the institute.

Baslovitch checked the instruments again, and through the windscreen he could see movement—two running men. They weren't wearing uniforms, but in their hands he could see weapons.

It was not the army or the KGB—it was the drug smugglers, Baslovitch realized.

Baslovitch was a devotee of espionage films— the spy stories where the Soviet agents were always incredibly evil and the Western agents incredibly good amused him greatly—and in these films aircraft could always get off the ground from a cold start in a matter of seconds. In real life, such was not the case.

He figured he'd have to wait at least another two minutes before he could even try.

Baslovitch reached to the seat beside him, opened his attaché case and extricated the Uzi, fitting it with one of the 32-round double-column boxes. Giving a final eye to the instruments, he was up and moving to the fuselage door.

Throwing it open, he shouted. "Hands in the air, and away from the plane." He worked the cocking handle of the Uzi rapidly for as loud a sound as possible as he dropped to the tarmac.

Neither man moved, nor raised his hands. Each held something Baslovitch now recognized—Czech Skorpion machine pistols. "I think not," the man to Baslovitch's right called back across the twenty yards that separated them.

Baslovitch mentally ticked off the seconds, deciding to play the uniform to the hilt. "You are both under arrest."

The one to Baslovitch's left laughed. "I don't think so. But you are in trouble, Comrade," he said.

Silently, Baslovitch agreed with them. Two submachine guns to one were not very good odds at all. And if the men survived, armed, they would shoot down the aircraft even if he could somehow get the wheel chocks away, get back into the cockpit and then get airborne. He decided on another approach. "Take your marijuana—I have no use for it. But I must use the aircraft—government business." That was in a way true—the business of eluding the government.

"Forget the aircraft and the marijuana, and we let you live." The voice was a new one, from behind him, and Baslovitch silently cursed himself.

Quickly, he said, "If there is gunplay, the aircraft may become so damaged that it cannot be flown, and your contraband will be discovered."

"Our guns are aimed at you, not at the aircraft," the man behind him said.

Baslovitch considered the remark and began to edge away from the aircraft. He could not afford for it to sustain damage either. Once the first shot was fired, the gate guards and any others on the field would rush to the spot, the authorities would be called and his new enemies would swarm over the field. There would be no time to find another aircraft and get it airborne.

Baslovitch kept edging left. "At least two of you will die. But no doubt you've considered this?" Baslovitch said, trying to buy time.

"More profit for those who live." It was the voice behind him. The two men he faced split wide right and left, and Baslovitch smiled. They were suddenly afraid that the man behind him wanted them dead as well.

Baslovitch kept edging left. There was very little chance he would make it alive. If he was to die, he decided, it might as well be spectacularly.

At the top of his lungs, he shouted, "In the plane—now!"

The eyes of the man nearest the plane shifted and Baslovitch twisted and dived forward, spraying the Uzi toward the darkness behind him. A long automatic burst of gunfire, like torchlight, silhouetted the voice from the darkness to the rear of the plane. Baslovitch's Uzi sliced laterally from left to right, cutting through the brilliant effect of the muzzle-flashes. Baslovitch twisted onto his abdomen, firing a short 3-round burst at the man nearest the aircraft. There was no time to check for a hit as he rolled across the tarmac, the tarmac beside him chewing up under automatic-weapons fire. Baslovitch's Uzi sprayed toward the source of the fire.

The Uzi's 32-round magazine was empty—but there was no returning gunfire.

Shaking, Baslovitch stood.

Three men lay dead in the airfield lights, and there were sure to be more men on the way, men who wouldn't bother to talk first. Baslovitch yanked the wheel chocks away and decided to get the hell away from the airfield.

BEHIND THE CONTROLS Baslovitch gunned the Antonov's engine. He needed one thousand horses and quickly.

The vibration grew stronger and the aircraft began moving forward. The three dead drug smugglers—Baslovitch had pushed one of the bales of marijuana onto the runway surface—would actually serve him. A drug deal gone wrong, the pilot of the stolen aircraft escaping after the shootout—likely the blond and mustachioed air force captain was the culprit.

The authorities would be looking for a smuggler and a killer, not an escaping KGB major.

He checked his flaps and airspeed—the fence at the far end of the field was coming up fast. And so were the emergency vehicles, flashers blooming in the night. Some of the occupants would be armed, and Baslovitch pushed open the storm vent, stabbing one of the H-Ks into the cold air and firing. One of the vehicles swerved, but the light was too poor and Baslovitch's aircraft was moving too fast for Baslovitch to be sure of a hit.

He dropped the pistol to the seat beside him as the fence raced toward him. He brought the engine to full revs and pulled back on the yoke with all his strength. There was a sudden bump and a lurch and he was airborne.

Sergei Nicolai Baslovitch white-knuckled the control yoke. There would be several minutes of low-level flying, avoiding trees, radio towers and maybe ground fire before he could lose himself and the aircraft in the darkness.

14

The flight from Khorog to Alma Ata had been almost boring, Track thought, except that Desiree had fallen asleep in his arms. The plan they had finally devised required a woman, and try as Track and Zulu had, neither had been able to discourage Desiree from taking the part, let alone forbid her.

The thought of what she had to do, and what might happen to her, made Track horribly uncomfortable. Prostitutes were brought in for some of the men interned for research purposes at the institute. Apparently the institute staff studied the men while they performed sex acts.

Disguised as a hooker, Desiree would be the only one of them to be allowed inside freely.

She might be searched, but only cursorily, and her presence inside the institute would allow for a two-pronged attack if the right guard could be found. That guard would be the one to search Desiree. If Chesterton was armed with a weapon and explosives and Desiree was armed, enough diversion could be created to allow Track and Zulu to penetrate the institute.

Hakim Mohammed's private business jet was preparing for landing, and Track awakened Desiree Goth.

She shook her head, stretching like a cat, smiling. Her black hair fell around her face and shoulders as she tossed her head, coming fully awake it seemed. For some odd reason, he thought of his cat, Dorothy, and his place in New Mexico.

After this thing at the institute was over, perhaps Desiree could get the few things he really wanted from the house and dispose of the rest, the house as well. Dan Track doubted if he would ever return to it. He wondered whether, if he ever left Russia alive, he would even make it back to the United States. It was a strange feeling, he thought.

"What did you say?" Desiree asked him.

"I didn't say anything," and he smiled at her. "Better buckle your seat belt." He didn't want to talk about what he was feeling. To rip his life out by the roots, to embark upon something that could only be described as foolhardy stupidity.

But for the first time in his life, Dan Track truly wanted blood. . . .

IT SEEMED AS THOUGH the million or so inhabitants of Alma Ata had all decided to crowd the streets with bicycles and cars at once. Desiree, between Track and Zulu in the back seat of the Mercedes, spoke of Alma Ata and her plan. "Once we have successfully got into the institute and out, I have an aircraft waiting that will fly us across the border into China. The Chinese owe me many favors and they expect us. I am doing a favor for them in return.'' Desiree opened her purse. Her right hand produced a camera the size of two cigarette lighters, silver toned. It was the classic spy camera of the movies. ''They want to know what is going on at the institute. I will hopefully be able to show them. With this.''

''Desiree is a lovely name for a spy,'' Track said as he smiled. ''But an amateur spy has about the same possibilities for success as an amateur brain surgeon.''

''But a woman is born to it,'' Desiree replied, returning his smile with one of her own as she dropped the camera back into her purse.

As if he was a tour guide, Zulu interrupted. ''The building there, with the cantilevered roof, is the Lenin Palace of Culture. In fact, Alma Ata is known throughout the Communist world as a center of culture—theater, music, dance. As well as the Kazakh Soviet Socialist Republic Academy of Sciences, there are three rather decent museums. The botanical gardens are quite lovely. And there is the opera house, of course. I once spent several weeks here with Mr. Mohammed. But there was time away from business to enjoy the splendors of the city. There is one curious thing which as non-Communists we cannot fully appreciate—a rather fascinating portrait of Lenin made from living foliage. Rather striking in its own way.''

''I'll try not to miss it,'' Track remarked.

Hakim Mohammed sat beside the chauffeur in the driver's compartment of the Mercedes and he turned to look back at them. "You would do well to heed Zulu, Major Track. The old expression— know thy enemy?" And then the Arab, looking quite at home in an off-white *keffiyeh* bound with a rope of gold at the forehead, turned away, saying nothing else. . . .

HAKIM MOHAMMED HAD ACQUIRED a house for their use, several miles beyond Alma Ata and near the mountains of the Tien Shan range. Several times during the drive from the city, Track had seen soldiers and been amazed at the deference paid to the Mercedes of Hakim Mohammed. There had been no interference and the vehicle was not stopped.

The house was flat-roofed and huge by anyone's standards. Track turned away from it, looking toward the mountains. Clouds were visible below the mountain peaks. "We fly over that?" Track asked Desiree, beside him.

He felt her hands grope for his right hand and he closed his fingers over hers. "Yes, after—"

"If, you mean," and Track looked at her.

"Yes, and if, then I will arrange for you to get back over the mountains into Russia itself."

"This will ruin your business contacts."

"I know—but I love you."

Track held her close to him. "Let's get started then," Dan Track told her.

TRACK WORKED the focal adjustment knobs on the Aimpoint 8x30s. Lying at the lip of a craggy drop, he swept the binoculars over the institute. Five flat-roofed, very modern single-level buildings formed the spokes of a wheel. Their center, at the hub of the wheel, was a sixth building, two-storied and with a peaked roof, the design bearing some similarity to a chalet, but vastly larger.

A high concrete wall surrounded the compound, perhaps two hundred yards from the farthest edges of the peripheral buildings, and atop the wall was barbed wire. Track could not read the Cyrillic signs posted at intervals on the wall, but he guessed that the red-and-white signs with the bold black lettering warned that the wire was electrically charged.

If all went well, at least on the way in, the wall would not be a difficulty. And on the way out, explosives could blow out a suitable chunk to use as an exit if necessary.

Hakim Mohammed had contacted the guard and made the arrangements, but that could always turn into a trap, Track knew. And he would know for sure tomorrow....

15

Morton Tillman sat in the darkened room, alone except for George Beegh. There had been some resistance to the drugs, but the threat of harming the young man's mother had eradicated that. And now the drugs had taken hold.

"George?"

"Yes, dad."

"Do you trust me, George?"

"Yes, dad."

"I appreciate your trust, George—because as we both know, your trust has at times been misplaced, hasn't it?"

"Yes, dad."

"Tell me about the man you trusted once—"

"Dan Track?"

"Yes. Tell me what he did."

"He isn't Dan Track," George began. "He killed mom's real brother when Dan was in the Army. And he tried to kill you and mom. And he's coming here now to kill both of you."

"That's right," Morton Tillman confirmed. "Are you going to let him do this, George?"

"No, I won't."

"But this man is very skilled and well armed."

"I can fight him. I can win."

"Would you kill him?"

There was no pause. Tillman jotted down a note—the response was excellent. The stronger drugs, the ones he had never dared try on Diane Beegh because they would kill her, worked marvelously with George.

"What about the Englishman, Chesterton?"

"He is in league with the man who calls himself Dan Track."

"What do you think you should do about him, George?"

"Kill him."

"That is an admirable sentiment, but he can be killed later. Why not just beat him up? That should be very easy for you. Now, tell me about the importance of my work here, George. Why it is important to the United States. Why, as a patriotic and loyal American you must help to assure that I complete it."

"You are training certain people who have demonstrated powers of telekinesis to disarm the Russians all at once and make the world safe."

"Explain how I utilize telekinesis, George."

"People who can bend spoons with their minds, or make pencils or pieces of paper move—with the drugs you have developed for the United States government you can amplify the power they have."

"And what will my test subjects do to all of the

missiles in the silos near Moscow, George?'' Tillman had merely substituted the word "Moscow" for the words "New York."

"Detonate them in their silos. The Russians will think it is some terrible accident."

"That's right—and then United States troops can march into East Germany and liberate the people there. What a good idea, to help humanity." Again, Tillman had told George the truth, merely substituting United States for Russia and East Germany for West. "So what must we do, if Dan Track makes it here? What will you do?"

"Kill him."

"Very good. I'll even trust you with a gun, George."

"Thanks."

"Now, why don't you show this Sir Abner Chesterton, this Soviet agent, just what to expect when the Russians try to get tough with America. When I say 'I'm proud of you, son,' you'll get up. The lights will go on and you'll walk out of the room with me and we'll go to the detention cell where Chesterton is being held. Then you'll beat him up."

"Yes, dad."

"I'm proud of you, son." Tillman hit the light switch, squinting against the light at the figure of George Beegh. He had restored the young man's watch and clothes, even the black Jack Daniels baseball cap. George stood up, and Tillman stood up with him. "Where are we going, George?"

"To beat the crap out of that rotten Commie bastard Chesterton."

Tillman opened the door, and George, his face set with hatred, walked ahead.

SIR ABNER CHESTERTON squinted against the light. The beam of a flashlight more powerful than any of the lights he had seen before was poking violently into his cell.

"Out," a thickly accented voice called.

Chesterton stood. His back ached and he was stiff despite the rigid exercise program he had begun since his interment—how many days ago was it? He had lost track of the time.

Limping slightly, he started from his cell, the light brighter still in the corridor. Through his half-closed eyes he thought he could see George.

"George? Is that you?" he asked.

"It's me, you fuckin' Commie—did you help that guy kill my real uncle and take his place?" And suddenly Chesterton felt something crash against his chest and he was sprawling back onto the cold tiled floor of the hallway.

His eyes were accustomed enough to the light now. George was hulking over him, his muscles bulging beneath the open front of his shirt. "George. What's wrong with you?" Chesterton shouted.

"Nothing, but plenty's going to be wrong with you." George's left hand flashed out, the fist knotting in the front of Chesterton's prison-style uniform. Chesterton felt himself being dragged to his feet, then lifted from them as George slammed his back against the wall. "I'm going to rip your damn arms off and beat you to death with them."

"George, you—" Chesterton saw it coming, trying to duck George's left hand, but as he ducked it, he doubled forward, bright yellow and green and red floaters in his eyes, his groin screaming with pain, his breath gone, his stomach heaving.

He was brought roughly to his feet. George's hands were on his shoulders, dragging him up. Pain sliced through his body as he straightened. George's right flashed out and Chesterton blocked it, trying to push George away, not wanting to strike his friend, but George's left hammered him in the cheek, slamming him back against the wall. George's right foot swung forward and Chesterton slumped away from it, the foot smashing into his left shoulder rather than his head or neck. Pain flooded over him again.

George was raising him bodily from the ground, hurtling him along the corridor.

"George! My God, man, what have they done to—"

Another kick, Chesterton taking it in the chest, rolling with it, slamming into the wall.

And George was on him now, straddling his chest. Chesterton couldn't breathe.

George's right fist cracked across the bridge of Chesterton's nose like a blackjack. Blood sprayed out over his face and chest. George hit him again and again, then suddenly Tillman's voice thundered out.

"That is enough, George."

"But—"

"Enough. You can kill the Englishman later." As George started to rise, Chesterton looked up. A hypodermic syringe was jabbed into George's left arm below the elbow. George sagged back against the wall, and Morton Tillman snapped his fingers and two guards came forward. "He'll sleep for twelve hours—take him," Tillman said in Russian.

Then Morton Tillman looked down and Chesterton's eyes met his. "What do you think, Sir Abner—do my drugs work, or don't they? When Dan Track comes here, George will believe that Track is not really his uncle at all. He'll believe that Track tried to kill his mother, tried to kill him—even tried to kill me. George's mother already believes her brother did these things. Diane will draw Track here, draw him to her like a moth is drawn to a candle flame. And then George will execute Track—how fitting."

Barely able to breathe, Chesterton pushed himself up into a sitting position against the wall. "Why?" he asked Tillman. "Why?"

Tillman shrugged his shoulders and smiled. "Why not? Track will come and he must be eliminated, why not serve the cause of science in the process, hmm?"

"Bastard!"

"It was interesting, don't you agree, to see how far George would go?"

"What do you plan to accomplish, other than satisfy your own perversions?"

"Perversions? Perhaps, but my reasons go beyond them. Tomorrow, less than twenty-four hours from now, Soviet divisions will be poised on the borders of West Germany. My experiments will bring the Soviet Union the greatest near-bloodless military victory of history. Tomorrow the men and women I have here—my 'wife' the most important of them—will focus their telekinetic skills. With the help of the drugs I have perfected over the past two decades, they will be of sufficient intensity that the nuclear missile silos near New York will suddenly erupt in flame as the warheads are triggered from within. With the millions of lives that will be lost, there will be a public outcry in the West for nuclear disarmament. The Americans will be too busy to bother about Germany. Tomorrow, the conquest of West Germany begins!"

"And the next day the world, Tillman? Like some third-rate movie villain?"

"Yes." Tillman laughed. "But not the next day—at least a few weeks. Once the effectiveness of my telekinetics has been proven, thousands of mentally sensitive prisoners will be brought to me and with their combined power under the influence of my drugs, I shall be capable of obliterating armies."

"Even the Soviet army, Tillman?"

And Morton Tillman smiled. "Perhaps—yes, perhaps." He walked down the corridor, telling the two remaining guards as he turned the corner, "Clean him up and lock him away. I don't want him bleeding to death just yet."

THE GUARD DRAGGED HIM into the cell and left the cell door open for a moment. Chesterton was too battered to attempt escape. Besides, where would he go? And the guard was armed. When the guard returned, he set his bright hand torch beside Chesterton on the floor of the cell and pulled the door closed. The man said in poor English, "I am a friend—here." Chesterton felt the shape that was pressed into his hands—it was a pistol, and fitted to the muzzle was something that could only have been a silencer.

"When the evening meal comes, you will kill your guards and escape into the corridor. I have drawn a map of the complex." Chesterton felt a piece of paper pressed into his right hand. The man washed Chesterton's face with a cool rag as he spoke. The pain was unbearable. But Chesterton fought to ignore it, trying to follow every word of the guard's whispered instructions. "I will leave you plastique—the map shows locations where you are to leave it."

"Who are you, why should I trust you?"

"The gun is loaded."

"That didn't answer my question."

"The man who paid me said to tell you that Major Track wants to pay you back for all the free meals before he joined the—I cannot remember the word—"

"Consortium," Chesterton whispered, and somehow the word sounded very far away.

"Yes. There are spare magazines for the pistol, six of them, along with the explosives and detonators in the bag I'll leave on the floor."

"When is Track coming?"

"Tonight, one half hour after your evening meal. You will have to hurry." The man stood up, picking up the lantern.

"Wait, I want to thank you—"

"I have been paid." The light started toward the door. Sir Abner Chesterton heard the guard murmur, "Good luck." Then the door was slammed and in the darkness Chesterton found the bag of tricks. He held the wet rag to the bridge of his nose, but the rag was no longer cool.

And in his right hand he held the pistol with the silencer. He was ready for dinner. Very ready.

MORTON TILLMAN PUT DOWN the telephone. Moscow.

The operation, so secret it had no code name, had been moved up by twelve hours to 7:00 A.M.

And Colonel Dmitri Jurgenov would be arriving in under two hours with one hundred handpicked members of special forces to supervise the security of the institute while the experiment was underway.

Tillman stood up, lighting his pipe. He walked across the room to stare at himself in a mirror. A good bit of gray salted his dark brown hair, and there were some lines around his eyes and mouth. His face was too thin. But all of this was from the years of study, the years of research.

Tomorrow morning rather than tomorrow night would be his hour.

He turned to view his profile in the mirror, and wondered what sort of statue would be built to him.

And he laughed at himself, murmuring to his reflection, "Larger than life!"

16

Desiree Goth had planned ahead, consulting with Hakim Mohammed, who owned the operation that delivered prostitutes to the institute. She sat naked now on the bed in the room she shared with Dan Track, staring at the clothes she would wear.

Soviet prostitutes, she decided, at least near Alma Ata, dressed very tackily.

She shrugged and stood up, inspecting the clothes again, throwing them down in disgust, then taking the lace-trimmed, black, see-through panties and pulling them on. She felt embarrassed wearing them. The black bra, if there was enough of it to be called a bra, closed in the front between her breasts. There were holes in the front of the cups for the nipples to protrude.

She pulled the garter belt, also black and trimmed with red lace, up along her thighs and to her waist. As she positioned it, she wondered if Hakim Mohammed had taken any perverse satisfaction in securing these clothes for her.

She sat on the edge of the bed. The black stockings were real silk—she imagined only a prostitute could afford them inside the Soviet

Union. She pulled them on, first the left, then the right.

Standing up, she secured the tops of the stockings to her garter belt.

She looked at herself in the mirror. *"Merde,"* she whispered.

She slipped into a red, sleeveless blouse, with a low-cut front and back, and then pulled on a black leather miniskirt that zipped up the front with an industrial-size zipper.

Then she stepped into a pair of black, stiletto-heeled shoes.

She looked at herself in the mirror. The makeup still had to be done, the hair arranged, the ghastly shade of nail polish applied. But already she looked the part.

She stepped back and laughed at herself—a millionairess who hooked as a hobby to help the man she loved.

"WHAT DO YOU THINK?"

Dan Track looked at her—the short leather skirt, the red blouse, the dark stockings—the red nails and lipstick, the excessive makeup, the hair done in tiny ringlets about her head. "Isn't it a little overdone?" he said.

"I should say just the opposite—the eyes still show their flare, their refinement, their wit," Zulu added.

"It is perfect, Miss Desiree," Hakim Mohammed interjected. Track looked at the Arab, and the Arab positively seemed to drool. Track made a mental note of what kind of woman Hakim Mohammed got turned on by.

"I think it needs boots and a whip, myself," Track told her, standing up.

"You think it looks bad, you should try wearing it," Desiree said as she smiled.

"I still don't like you doing this, there's got to be another—"

"There is no other way," Desiree said. "Besides, if Hakim's friend did the first half of his job, I'll have two confederates inside to assist me." And she walked toward the center of the room and leaned forward to pick up a revolver and a holster from the coffee table. She checked the Smith & Wesson Model 60's cylinder, then closed it and placed the two-inch snubby revolver back on the coffee table. She picked up the holster, then hitched up her skirt, and putting her left foot on the coffee table, buckled the thigh holster to the inside of her left leg with Velcro closures. Then she reached up her skirt and secured the alligator clip that served as the vertical support for the holster. To what she secured it, Track could only conjecture.

Holstering the gun, Desiree put her foot down, smoothing what little there was of her skirt along her thighs. "Does it show?"

"No," Track told her. "But I'd be careful sitting down."

"I will," she replied, smiling. She picked up the

black leather shoulder bag from the coffee table, opening it. First one, then a second Walther P-5 emerged from the bag, one of them silencer-fitted. "Did either of you check these?" Desiree asked, looking from Track to Zulu.

"I did," Track answered. "Both are chamber-loaded with full magazines. You have six spare magazines in the shoulder bag—it might be a bit heavy to carry."

"I'll endure it," she said with a smile.

She replaced both pistols in the bag, laying them gently on top of the plastique and detonators that Mohammed had supplied, then set the bag back on the coffee table.

Track watched her as she walked toward him. She was practicing her hooker walk, her hips moving with exaggerated motion. She stopped inches from him. With the six-inch heels she wore, her eyes were almost level with his. She handed him her watch. "You keep this. Hakim has a cheap flashy wristwatch for me that goes with the outfit."

Track took the watch, and then he folded his arms around her. He was afraid for her—and for himself if she died.

DESIREE HAD GONE ON AHEAD, as she was supposed to do. He had kissed her, held her for a long time and then watched as Hakim had driven her to the rendezvous point with the pimp who serviced the institute. Track had gone inside quickly after

the car had vanished down the roadway, to pre-
pare for his own part of the mission. He changed
from the gray slacks into a pair of faded Levi's,
from crew socks of dark gray to black boot socks,
from loafers—all the civilized clothes supplied by
Hakim Mohammed back at the Chinese house—to
black Vietnam-era combat boots. The Nam boots
were increasingly hard to find and someday, he
supposed, he'd have to have them custom-made.
He used O.D. blousing garters with the Levi's to
secure them just at the top of his boots.

He checked the cylinder on his S&W .357, gave
it a good-luck spin and secured it in a Bianchi
shoulder rig, then slipped the holster in place. He
picked up his Trapper Scorpion and saw that the
chamber was loaded. Lowering the hammer gently
over the chambered round, he placed the gun in
the Alessi hide-a-holster, then placing gun and
holster behind his right kidney.

In the breast pocket of his dark blue snap-front
shirt he placed a Scribe, a trick felt-tip pen that
concealed a triangular blade. He checked his
gloves—the back of each held three of his custom-
made stainless-steel Shuriken throwing spikes. He
slipped a boot knife inside the waistband of his
Levi's under his wide leather belt, and jammed a
Puma lock-blade folding knife in the front pocket
of his Levi's. His ordinary things like money,
keys, wallet had been left with Faring-Brown and
Track assumed they were somewhere in Switzerland now.

Track pulled on his battered, brown leather bomber jacket, the side patch pockets bulging with shot shells and slug loads for the SPAS-12. He slung the two Norwegian army engineers' bags to his frame, cross-body, one on each side, one loaded with more ammunition for the shotgun, the other loaded with spare magazines for the Trapper Scorpion and Safariland Speed Loaders for the L-Frame Smith.

He was traveling heavy enough—no submachine gun, no assault rifle.

Track pulled on his special skintight gloves with the Shuriken throwing spikes.

He lied when he looked at his image in the mirror—he told himself that he was ready.

ZULU STUDIED his reflection. The creases in his black BDU were razor-sharp.

Slung over the fatigue jacket and beneath his right armpit in a black ballistic-nylon holster was his Browning GP, the one he always carried when he carried at all. On the black leather belt at his waist were two Milt Sparks Four-Packs with a total of eight 13-round magazines for the Hi-Power. He thought of the story of the defenders again—the old men and boys who had saved his tribe from slaughter ages in the past—as he withdrew the black cat's-paw-handled stainless-steel Gerber Mark 2 from his belt sheath. It was not a sword but it was, after all, the spirit that counted.

Another identical Gerber was suspended at his right side.

He took up his two black musette bags. One held spare magazines for the Walther MPK submachine gun he would carry into battle; the other, spare shells for his SPAS-12 shotgun.

As he adjusted the black woolen watch cap to his head at a slightly rakish angle, he reflected that black was the color of death. He had always prided himself on dressing appropriately for the occasion.

He picked up the SPAS and the Walther MKP and walked out of his room.

DAN TRACK SMOKED one of the Cuesta-Rey Six-Ts. He heard the door open and close behind him. "You ready, Zulu?" he asked without looking.

"An absurd question, Major," the reply came back.

"For once I agree with you," Track told him. "But just this once."

Hakim Mohammed's Mercedes had returned ten minutes ago, and Track started down from the porch toward it. Zulu strode beside him.

17

Desiree Goth had not spoken with the man Hakim
Mohammed had left her with. No names had been
given on either side. No prostitutes were expected
at the institute for any testing purposes, and so
Desiree rode alone in the ancient Volkswagen
microbus. For some reason, she sat with her knees
so tight together that they physically ached, but
she would not move them. She had stared at the
photos of Diane Beegh and Robert Beegh, stared
at them long enough to memorize every facial detail, listened as Dan Track had told her the most
intimate of details regarding Diane, listened too as
Hakim had droned out every detail that could be
obtained regarding the layout of the institute.

Her makeup case was packed with various jars
of creams and lotions, all of them holding plastic
explosives. Her mission at the institute was two-
fold—to utilize the explosives as part of the diversion that would allow Track and Zulu to get into
the institute, and then to proceed to the living
quarters of the institute and find Diane Beegh and
keep her safe.

The Volkswagen's transmission rattled and the

brakes squealed, and she leaned forward to peer over the driver's shoulder through the windshield. A large crack in the right side of the glass distorted the gateway beyond and the two guards there, making their bodies bent and twisted.

The driver jerked his right thumb toward the side door of the Volkswagen and Desiree stared at him a moment, unaccustomed to having to open a car door or any door for herself. But she shrugged and resigned herself to it, working the interior door handle and getting out, awkwardly because of the tightness of the leather miniskirt. She slammed the door closed behind her. Hakim Mohammed had said the guard she should see had a knife scar on his left cheek. But neither of these men near the front gate had such a scar. She hesitated.

There was a third guard running up to the gates and the other two turned as he called out to them, one of the first two guards laughing. She noticed the scar on the left cheek of the third guard, jagged, pink, almost wet looking. And she noticed the superior rank ensignia he wore on his uniform. She tried not to look relieved. She waited another ten seconds as she counted them out and walked ahead, her best hip swivel at high gear, toward the scar-faced guard.

The man with the scar, a corporal, stepped toward her, shooing the other two men to their guardhouse by the gate. He walked beside her as she followed him through the gate. He started into the second of the smallish guardhouses—about the size of a large bathroom and made of stone. The other two guards waited outside the first guardhouse, the one who had laughed before laughing again.

The scar-faced corporal of the guard closed the door behind them, locking it.

"So, you are the one they wish inside."

"Yes," she answered in Russian.

"They pay a good amount—you are important?"

"Yes, I am important."

"Pay me something first." He reached out and his right hand insinuated itself against the base of her left breast through the open front of her short, black leather jacket.

Desiree didn't move his hand or try to step away. Coldly, quietly, she told him, "You will get the gold—I am the one paying it. Remove your hand and let me inside or you'll never get an ounce of it. Betray me, and you will be betrayed."

She looked from his eyes to his hand, then back to his eyes.

His hand moved away and the pressure against her left breast was gone.

"We must wait a few moments longer—they must think that I—"

"I understand." She sat on the edge of the desk, took out a cigarette and held it to her lips, looking at the scar-faced guard. "I'm waiting."

He stepped forward, fumbled in his pockets for a moment, then struck a match. She put the tip of the cigarette into the flame, smelling the phosphorous as she inhaled, then exhaled the smoke quickly as she murmured, "Thank you."

Desiree Goth owned the situation, knew that she did and used the knowledge. . . .

SERGEI NICOLAI BASLOVITCH studied the terrain through his armored Zeiss binoculars. It was imperative that he intercept Dan Track prior to Track's entering the institute. It would be a solitary task. He had spent two days and one night camped in the foothills, watching. There had been the telltale glint of binoculars the previous day, and by the time he had reached the spot of origin, there had been no one. Some marks on the ground, but they could have been nothing. The possibility existed that Track had tried entering the area surrounding Alma Ata earlier and failed. Or that Track had been intercepted and killed. That Track would not attempt to follow up the evidence that his sister might still be alive did not seriously enter Baslovitch's mind. Track was too much like Baslovitch himself not to.

If there had been a raid on the institute, Baslovitch could have read it, he told himself. There was no guard activity beyond what he had expected there would be. There were no signs of damage. In the town of Alma Ata itself, there were no additional patrols, no random checks for papers. Life was as normal.

Which meant Track had not come yet.

Baslovitch had no choice but to wait. He could

hide in the foothills for weeks. But eventually, if Track did not come, he would have to try the border crossing himself.

China was out of the question. The border was too heavily guarded and he had no desire to defect to the Chinese. It would be Afghanistan—where everyone would count him an enemy. The Russians would pursue him, and the Afghans would consider him Russian.

To steal a plane in such a closely guarded city as Alma Ata—missile installations and the like—would be exceedingly difficult, and crossing the border with radar searching for him would be all but impossible.

What escape route Track had, Baslovitch could not guess. But he felt certain it had to do with the tempestuously lovely Desiree Goth. Her smuggling operations reached inside Soviet territory—Baslovitch had long known this, but he had always felt that smugglers who did not deal in drugs or white slavery had a certain charm to them, and Desiree Goth dealt in neither. And she certainly possessed an abundance of charm.

It would be Desiree Goth who had the route constructed to get Track and whoever was with him to safety.

And if it was a route into China, Baslovitch would take his chances with Track and the Chinese.

Baslovitch brought the Zeiss binoculars to his eyes again, scanning the vantage points overlooking the institute, looking for Dan Track and for escape from the land he had served and now somehow was coming to feel strangely different about....

SIR ABNER CHESTERTON could breathe only through his mouth. His nostrils were clotted with blood, his nose stiff. To try to free his nasal passages would only have been to start the bleeding again.

He did not blame George—he blamed Morton Tillman and his drugs.

According to his biological clock, it was dinnertime. He had checked the silenced pistol, still not trusting the guard. There was a slide lock on it and he left it raised, giving himself just one shot.

He had killed during the days in the Royal Commandos, killed too working with Dan Track for the Consortium. He had never actually pointed a loaded gun at someone and wished a life away. Even garroting a German soldier had been combat. This—and he did not delude himself—was murder.

But he was prepared to commit it.

One guard would open the door and wait outside, whistling as he usually did. The second guard would walk inside with the light bulb and the flashlight, check that the prisoner was sufficiently docile and then use the flashlight to screw in the light bulb.

The bulb in place, the guard would go outside and return with the tray of what could barely be called food.

If Chesterton waited for the light, it might temporarily blind him.

In the semidarkness from the torch, Chesterton could see more clearly than the guard. He would do it then, lower the slide lock, cycle the action, up the slide lock and step into the corridor and kill the second guard. That would be less like murder, for this second man would be armed. The guard who brought the meal was never armed.

Chesterton waited, his right fist closed tightly on the butt of the pistol.

He heard the customary bang on the door—politeness, he wondered, in case he was defecating or something?

Chesterton heard the key turn in the lock and moved the pistol beneath his right thigh to obscure it. He squinted his eyes tight in preparation for the beam from the flashlight and the back light from the corridor.

The door opened, and Chesterton could smell fresh air as it invaded his cell.

Chesterton squinted against the light. In his bad English, the guard said, "You should have let the boy kill you, Englishman."

Chesterton groaned as if in pain, and since his nose ached, his cheek ached, his groin ached and his back ached, it required no acting.

The light splayed across him and he recoiled

from it. The guard laughed. "You should see the face on your head—very bad."

Chesterton groaned again and the light moved away.

Chesterton found the pistol by touch, and gripped the butt.

He could make out the outline of the guard as the flashlight shone on the ceiling and the bulb was screwed in place.

Chesterton raised the pistol.

He could not shoot someone in the back. "Turn around, you Communist bastard," Chesterton croaked, his throat dry, his nose completely clogged.

The Communist guard turned, his booted right foot swinging out. Chesterton shot him in the right eye. He'd aimed for the left.

As the body fell forward, Chesterton lurched out of the way.

He was up and at the door, just as the second guard was coming through, an AKM in his hands at high port.

Chesterton fired into the guard's wide-open mouth and the body slammed back. As if in slow motion, Chesterton saw the man's right hand twitch. Would it touch the trigger of the AKM? Would the rifle fire? Others would come.

He would be caught.

But the rifle did not discharge.

Chesterton picked up the rifle and slung it across his back. Then he turned and went back into the cell and picked up the bag containing the spare magazines for the pistol, the plastique and the map of the places to position the charges.

He turned his back on his cell—he would never return to it. He would either ensure his freedom from this place, or he would die.

In the corridor, he changed magazines in the pistol to give himself a full eight rounds plus the one in the chamber.

And he checked his plastique, the simplest and most space-effective of charges. He had used similar charges with the old red Deta sheet material more years ago than he wanted to remember. The red Deta sheet had been unstable, but this more modern version was not—he hoped. It was olive drab in color and approximately three-eighths of an inch thick; the width was just under three inches. Self-adhesive backings—in the old days he had used rubber cement. Six non-electric blasting caps and six small plastic bags of what he assumed to be smokeless powder were in the bottom of the bag.

He had known an American agent during the days of World War II who had loved such simple explosive techniques for their subtlety. The man had often remarked "Waste not, want not," while taking some perfectly ordinary materials and turning them into devastating explosives.

Chesterton searched the body of the dead guard in the corridor and came up with two spare magazines for the AKM. Then he set rifle and magazines and pistol down on the corridor floor and shoved the cart loaded with food into his cell. He declined to eat any of it, despite his hunger. He dragged the body of the guard from the corridor toward the entrance of the cell, getting the body up against the wall and shoving it in. He pushed the dead man's feet in the cell with the door itself as he closed it, locked it, then put the keys into his bag.

Taking up the rifle, the two spare magazines and the silenced pistol, Chesterton started down the corridor. He already knew the site of his first explosive charge. And for the first time in a long time, he felt alive.

DESIREE GOTH LEANED up and planted a kiss on the cheek of the corporal, to keep up his image with the other two guards. A totally defeated person was a potentially irrational enemy. It was why she had waited twenty minutes with him inside the stone guardhouse, and now, as she walked into the compound, she made a show of adjusting her clothing.

Ahead of her was the nearest of the five outer buildings. It was the reception center and Desiree walked toward it. She would be expected to.

There was more activity in the place than she had witnessed before spending the twenty minutes chain-smoking in the guardhouse with the scar-faced corporal, who was destined to be a very rich man thanks to her.

She climbed the three steps fronting the reception building and pulled on the double glass doors.

They were locked as they should be at this time of night. She knocked on the door to her right with the back of her right hand. There was some light filtering from beyond the doors.

No one answered, which was as she had hoped. Looking behind her, she took a flat sliver of plastic about the size of her American Express card—she had left home without it—and inserted it in the jamb between the two glass doors. The latch clicked and she let herself in, closing the door behind her.

Desiree Goth exhaled hard.

The first charge was to go beneath the top of the metal reception desk. It would turn the desk into a fragmentation grenade of gigantic proportions and blow out all the glass at the front of the building, Zulu had told her. Her own experience with plastique made her agree. There was no one coming and she moved behind the desk, dropping to her silk-stockinged knees. She removed one of the baseball-size chunks of C-4 from her purse and affixed it to the desk's underside, where the desk top met the front of the twin pedestal desk.

She set the electric blasting cap at the base of the charge, taking one of the dry-cell triple-A batteries from her purse and affixing it to the blasting cap with wires. Next, she took out one of the half dozen modified wristwatches she carried and pried open the back with a fingernail file. Then she ran wire leads from the battery to the watch.

She had been chewing gum—part of her image—and she reached into her mouth and removed it now, putting the piece behind the watch, securing the watch beneath the desk top.

Still on her knees, the charge set, she took another piece of gum from her purse and began chewing it—she hated gum, it made her jaw ache.

She was up and moving, down the corridor. There were more charges to set.

DAN TRACK AND ZULU stepped out of the Mercedes as Hakim Mohammed said to them, "Allah be with you both, I mean this."

Track nodded and shut the door, then followed Zulu in a jog from the edge of the road into the tree line. Without stopping, he started up through the trees toward the higher rocks that would lead to his selected vantage point overlooking the institute.

As they walked, Zulu whispered, "You seem of singular purpose today, Major."

"They have my sister Diane, they have George, they have Chesterton, and Desiree's inside by now. All the people I care about—yeah, I've got a purpose all right."

"I have yet to understand you, Major. You seem relaxed, almost flippant, yet there is an intensity lurking beneath the surface."

"Was that a compliment?"

"Merely an observation."

"Right," and Track stepped over a deadfall tree

and kept moving, the SPAS-12 extended ahead of him, tensioned against its sling.

SERGEI BASLOVITCH STARED intently through his binoculars at the gates of the institute.

He had seen the face, a face he recognized.

He had heard the noise of the choppers coming in, watched as they landed just beyond the perimeter of the institute itself. He had watched as the men, Soviet special forces troops, had disembarked and the helicopters had gone airborne again.

But the face of the leader haunted him. Baslovitch knew the face well.

There were men in every place, in every profession, who were animals.

This face belonged to one such man, Colonel Dmitri Jurgenov.

Jurgenov was a colonel in two armies, one the uniformed army within an army that was the Soviet special forces elite. The second was the silent army to which Baslovitch himself belonged. Had belonged. The KGB.

Either Track was expected very soon or some important work was about to take place.

Baslovitch estimated one hundred personnel had arrived to supplement the institute guard force. Machine guns were being put into position. Jurgenov was moving about the grounds of the institute, apparently issuing orders. Jurgenov liked that.

And then Baslovitch heard the noise behind him, the snap of a twig. He rolled, his right hand grasping the Uzi, but it was too late. And then he laughed.

"I'M GOING TO ASK you to do something for me, George."

"Yes, dad?"

"Two of the guards have been killed, and the Englishman has escaped. He's somewhere in the institute, we know that. I want you to find him; you alone know how he thinks. Find him, kill him—before he can help the man pretending to be Dan Track murder your mother."

"Yes."

"Here is a gun. Now go and get him. He's armed with a gun and an assault rifle. You didn't know this, George, but the one dead guard was a husband and father. He leaves a widow and three young children—little more than babies. The Englishman needs to be stopped!"

"Yes, dad."

The dead guard was, Morton Tillman thought, a once convicted rapist who had been paroled into the army and enjoyed beating people. Tillman had used his services more than once. The man had had a wife but she had left him after being nearly beaten to death during a drunken rage. Tillman reflected that he was only stretching the truth, and with the drugs, truth was what he made of it.

George opened his belt and slipped the holster

for the .45 onto it, then rethreaded the belt. Tillman watched as George automatically checked the loaded condition of the gun. Tillman knew nothing of firearms. The human mind was the ultimate weapon. This was just the beginning.

Apparently satisfied, George said, ''I'm ready.''

''Your mother and I are very proud of you, son. After you kill the Englishman, would you like to see your mother?''

''Yes, dad.''

''Go to the corridor where you beat the Englishman, follow him from there. The guards know you are helping us to find him.''

George Beegh nodded and walked from the room, picking up his black baseball cap with the whiskey advertisement on the front and pulling it low over his forehead.

Morton Tillman smiled.

18

"I found myself not overly fond of one major—now it appears I have two," Zulu announced, sitting down on a flat rock. Track watched him, then looked back to Baslovitch.

"What the hell are you doing here?"

"I fell onto hard times and was hoping to bum a ride—in the most basic terms."

Track dropped into a crouch on the ground beside Baslovitch and Zulu. The three men formed a triangle, Zulu perched on the rock at its apex.

"Your good intentions toward Major Track brought you into hard times?" Zulu asked.

Baslovitch looked at Zulu and shrugged. "My own people are trying to kill me—apparently they found out what I told Dan." Then Baslovitch looked at Track and grinned almost sheepishly. "That's what I get, I guess, for trying to do someone a good turn."

"I owe you," Track replied. "What do you want?"

"If you are going in, I assume you have a way of going out. I want to come along."

Track looked at Zulu, Zulu nodded. Track

looked back at Baslovitch. "No problem. But inside the institute they've got my sister, they've got George and they've got Sir Abner Chesterton. Desiree's also inside trying to get them out."

"And your brother-in-law?"

"I think I'm going to kill him."

"You'll have one hundred crack special-forces troops to deal with. I forgot to mention that. They just arrived. Their leader is a man named Colonel Dmitri Jurgenov. His brutality cannot be described."

"Where is your commitment—I mean, are you just saving your skin?"

Baslovitch's eyes flickered toward Zulu, then back to Track. He lit a cigarette with an old lighter and then said, "I am a Communist by birth and by choice. I have seen some things done in the name of the Party that even I find hard to accept. I have strong doubts, very strong doubts, that my government truly represents the will of my people. And I am ashamed to admit that I have been an instrument in their repression."

Track stared at Baslovitch as the Russian KGB major finished his speech. "After this is all over," he said, sweeping his arm in the direction of the institute, "I'm coming back. I'm going after the people who make misery. I'm going to cause them misery, more than they ever thought was possible. I'm not a killer, but—"

"Miss Desiree has spoken of this to me," Zulu interrupted. "She requested that I, ah—"

"That you what?" Track asked. "Baby-sit me? Change my diapers? Keep me from getting killed?"

"It is suicide, Major," Baslovitch said, raising his eyebrows. "But it might be fun. Tell me, if I'm not assuming too much, will three be company or a crowd?"

Track looked from Baslovitch to Zulu and back to Baslovitch again. "Welcome aboard, Sergei," he said.

19

Desiree Goth threw herself down as the sound of the last explosion reached her.

Then she picked herself up off the corridor floor and started to run. The building at the rear of the compound was her destination, the living quarters for the director and his wife and their upper echelon staff.

She was at the door, then through it, carelessly opening it because alarms were already sounding.

And then she saw him.

"George! George! It's me, Desiree!"

George Beegh turned to face her. In his hand was a .45 automatic. George was not only free, but armed as well. She started to say something to him, then stopped, her mouth open in astonishment. George had raised the pistol, and started to fire. She threw herself away from him and ran. She couldn't get over it—George was trying to kill her!

SIR ABNER CHESTERTON poured out the last of the smokeless powder and touched a match to it. It was the last charge, and a quick run along the corridor of the detention building would set the other charges.

The powder sparked, flamed for an instant, then hissed as a bright trail raced toward the Deta sheet on the far wall.

He couldn't wait to see it—it would blow out the wall.

Soldiers stormed in at the far end of the corridor. "Wait!" one shouted in English.

Chesterton brought his silenced pistol up and fired, all in one smooth motion, killing the man with two shots to the chest. Then he ran, as automatic weapons fire tore into the wall inches from his head.

As he ran, he could see the last three charges, all linked to one main powder trail. The trail branched off into three segments, each segment leading to a nonelectric blasting cap placed perpendicular to the edge of the self-adhesive Deta sheet, and all three charges placed, as Chesterton calculated it, to bring down the central wing of the building.

Chesterton reached the base of the three charges, flicking the match against the sandpaper striking surface and touched it to the powder.

Behind him, the gunfire was drowned out by a deafening roar, and he threw himself down, his breath gone.

His nose was bleeding again.

Chesterton pushed himself to his feet. The automatic weapons fire was gone. Acrid smoke filled the corridor, and the end of the hallway was illuminated with the orange glow of fire.

He ran, the glass in the far wall his nearest exit. He swung the AKM forward on its sling, pumping the trigger, emptying half a magazine, the glass disintegrating outward as Chesterton jumped, leaping through, sagging to his knees.

"Too old for this, Abner," he told himself.

He was up, running again but not very fast.

A woman was running toward him from the far side of the complex. There was something familiar about her, but she was dressed all wrong. In her garish clothes she had the look of a prostitute in a lower-class neighborhood. She was staring at him. He moved the rifle in his right hand, raising it slightly above his head.

"No, Sir Abner!" The woman almost screamed the words, running from him.

Desiree.

Chesterton shouted, "Get down—the building is going!"

He threw himself onto the dirt and saw Desiree do the same as he buried his head beneath his arms.

His ears registered the three simultaneous explosions and then began to ring and echo with the dull sound of crashing waves. He looked up to see flying debris; chunks of concrete rained down, accompanied by burning fragments of human bodies.

He ran, lurching toward Desiree Goth as she scrambled to her feet.

"Don't run from me, Desiree!" he shouted.

"No! You're like George!" she screamed back.

"My God, he's after you too?" Chesterton exclaimed.

"What—"

"No time. Let's get to the residential building."

Desiree stared up at him. "Your face—" she began.

"George. I'm pleased I was still recognizable. That man, Robert Beegh, is using drugs to turn George against us."

"Bastards!" a voice shouted from behind them. Chesterton turned to see George marching like an automaton past the flaming building, his face tinged red like the devil from the glow of the flames. He held a pistol in each hand.

Chesterton shoved Desiree ahead and ran.

"SET THAT SIDE of the net," Track shouted to Baslovitch. "Zulu, get her started!"

Track yanked at it, pulling camouflage net down.

"Where the hell did you get a T-72 MBT?" Baslovitch asked.

"Desiree. But don't ask where she got it," Track replied as he worked at his side of the net, looking up as Zulu climbed into the hatchway and down the turret into the nearly forty-ton main battle tank. Track's side of the camouflage netting away, he started up toward the turret.

"It's going to be crowded inside—usually just a commander and a gunner," Baslovitch said.

"We'll all hold our breath and keep our hands

to ourselves,'' Track called back as the Russian scrambled aboard.

Track beat Baslovitch to the hatch and climbed inside. Zulu was already seated in the commander's chair. "A wonderful machine, Major—independent fire control system, just the push of a button.''

Baslovitch, sliding behind Track, said, "It's a little more difficult than that, but you've got the spirit of the thing. The armor on these is the Chobham type—you Brits developed it.''

"I'm not a Brit, I'm African, Major Baslovitch.''

"Right. It's charge-resistant, at least that's what they say. I saw those special forces troops setting up a one-hundred-millimeter T-12 antitank gun out there—so let's hope the armor is as good as they say.''

"We're rolling—straight for the front door should be the perfect spot,'' Zulu called.

Track slid into the gunner's seat, but Baslovitch touched him on the shoulder and said, "Let me in there. You just enjoy the ride.''

Track gave up his seat.

MORTON TILLMAN forced the sounds of the explosions from his mind, talking instead in the darkened room to the twenty sensitives, his "wife" among them.

"The enemy is very strong and wishes to harm us—these sounds you hear are caused by the enemy." He prided himself on turning adversity to advantage. "We must defend our homes, our loved ones. And we alone can do this by seeing the missiles in their silos, by seeing the detonation systems. We must concentrate. We must focus our mental energies together. We must defeat these horrible enemies. Tell them, Janet." His wife, sitting in the dark beside him, seemed to move.

And then she spoke.

"I see the detonators, I see them. They are cold and dark. I will warm them. I will warm them." It was like a chant and another voice took it up. "I will warm them," and still another. "I will warm them," and still another, "I will warm them. I will warm them."

Tillman closed his eyes. It was only a matter of time now. Time and energy. He would miss Diane Beegh. The drugs had already taken their toll and soon the other drugs that held back their work would no longer be effective and she would die.

It was the one problem with the drugs he had begun so patiently to develop even before meeting the real Robert Beegh, before interesting the KGB in Beegh's work, before kidnapping Beegh and draining his mind.

He had personally executed Beegh when the American's mind was gone and Beegh was of no further use.

Tillman realized that his drug reached beyond the known levels of human mental capabilities, tapping something dark that in all of the years of experimentation he had never been able to fathom, tapping something that should not have been there but was, something that extended the human mind beyond the known limit.

The only unfortunate thing was the devastating side effect of the drug. For some reason it encouraged the growth of cancerous cells in the cerebral cortex.

Diane's body could not tolerate much more of the painkiller he had been giving her for more than a year. He estimated that she would die within another few weeks—her last brain scan had shown how far the cancer cells had infected her.

"Oh, well," he murmured under his breath.

The chant went on. "I will warm them," and by microdegrees he knew, in silos surrounding New York City, the most powerful city in the most powerful rival of his adopted country, explosive charges in missile detonators were slowly getting hot.

20

"George! Get back, George!"

Chesterton raised the AKM, firing a 3-round burst into the ceiling over George's head as the young man advanced down the corridor. George fired, a bullet from the .45 in his right hand ripping a chunk out of the corner of the hallway. Chesterton ducked back. "Run for it—that way," Chesterton said to Desiree. "I'll try to hold him off."

"You wouldn't—" He saw Desiree's eyes look at the assault rifle.

"No, I wouldn't. Now, run for it."

Sir Abner Chesterton almost shoved Desiree away from him, and Desiree ran down the main corridor of the residential building. Chesterton stabbed the AKM around the corner, firing high. Ducking his head around, he saw that George was gone.

Chesterton exhaled, a long sigh of relief. He leaned against the door frame nearest him, suddenly feeling it give way behind him. He threw his weight forward, twisting his head, craning his neck to see. George came through the doorway, his right hand grasping Chesterton's AKM, his left hand hammering out. Chesterton let go of the rifle, ducked and ran after Desiree Goth. There was only one way to stop George short of finding some antidote for the drugs Morton Tillman had given him, and that was to kill him.

Chesterton couldn't bring himself to do that— yet.

"THERE IS A TANK COMING. Comrade Colonel, one of our tanks, a T-72!"

Dmitri Jurgenov shouted orders to the two squads of men he had dispatched to the main building at the hub of the wheel, where Tillman was using his wife as the medium to activate the mental sensitives. "No one goes inside that building, no one but me! Hurry!"

He wheeled, running toward the main gate now, the excited lieutenant shouting as the man ran beside him. "It should not be here, Comrade Colonel!"

"But it is, idiot!"

He could see the tank himself now, rumbling down out of the foothills toward the gates at what seemed close to full speed—fifty miles per hour. The turret was moving, searching.

He could see the seven-man crew of the T-12 setting up to fire the 100mm antitank gun.

The T-72 battle tank fired first. Jurgenov threw himself to the ground, a shower of dirt and debris falling around him, the screams of his men filling the air. "Get that tank! Follow me!"

He was up and running, ripping a Czech CZ-75 9mm from his canvas flap holster. A weapon in his hands was a necessity, even though he knew the pistol was less than useless against the tank. "RPGs—get a team with me," he shouted to the lieutenant.

The T-12 fired, smoke and a tongue of flame belching from it in the darkness; the tank rocked but kept moving. "Damn!" Jurgenov had the RPG team with him now. "As close as you can, follow me!" Then he shouted over his shoulder to the lieutenant, "Organize the defense of the main gate if the tank should get past us. Hurry, man!"

The tank was closing in on the gates, and Jurgenov urged his men forward against it with threats and shouts and kicks. The distance to the tank now was some two hundred yards. "RPGs—fire at will!" he ordered.

Jurgenov dropped to one knee some distance behind the six privates with their rocket-propelled grenade launchers. One, then two more, then the next three fired in waves, all six stabilized missiles making smoking contrails toward the T-72. The T-72 was firing as well now, and Jurgenov threw himself to the ground. The scream of the 125mm gun made his ears ring, and he looked behind him—the gate was gone, and so were the men guarding it.

The RPG rounds exploded, and Jurgenov squinted as dust and debris rained down on him, but the T-72 was still coming. "Utilize the high-explosive antitank rounds—another ripple volley! Hurry!''

He wondered if his men could hear him, the noise of the T-72's 700bhp diesel was deafening. He took a radio from the corporal beside him, depressed the Talk button, and shouted, "This is Jurgenov—headquarters, come in. Under fire from T-72 tank. Using RPGs and our T-12. No good. T-72 closing toward main gates. Heavy losses. Need air support. Over!''

As the voice started to crackle back, Jurgenov threw himself to the ground again, the T-72's 7.62mm coaxial-mounted HMG firing, the ground around him plowing upward, the screams of dying men filling his ears.

He looked up—the radio lay shattered beside him.

Three men remained, including his corporal. Jurgenov grabbed up an RPG and then another, hurtling it into the arms of his corporal. He shouted to the corporal and the other two men, "When I give the signal, fire HEAT rounds aimed where the turret meets the tank body. Ready!''

One of the men screamed. The tank was less than a hundred yards away now. The soldier ran forward to rescue a wounded comrade, throwing down his RPG.

Jurgenov picked up his CZ-75 from the ground beside him, aimed the pistol at the fleeing man and shot him six times in the back. The man's body flopped on the ground like a fish out of water and then lay still. Jurgenov rammed the pistol into his holster, shouldered the RPG and shouted, "Fire, now!"

His rocket launcher kicked hard against his right shoulder, and he discarded it, edging back on his haunches, watching the three smoking contrails. The T-72 stuttered, almost stopped as first one then the two other missiles slammed into the front of the tank body where they would do the least good.

The T-72 kept coming, the 7.62mm HMG opening up again.

"Stay here!" Jurgenov commanded. "Use your rifles, fire at them!"

Jurgenov was up and running, hearing the renewed shriek of the T-72's 125mm gun, the whistle deafening him as he threw himself to the ground. He felt the rain of dirt and looked up—the entire front of the fence was gone.

He looked behind him. His two men were dead, crushed. The T-72 was rolling unhindered toward him.

Jorgenov pushed himself up and ran at a right angle to the tank toward the foothills. It was that or die.

DAN TRACK PUSHED OFF the quick employment safety of the SPAS. The tank shuddered around him as Zulu shouted, "We've crossed what's left of the wall—very little resistance now."

"I'm going out," Track shouted back over the

roar of the diesels. "Sergei, take charge of the tank, keep everybody busy. Zulu!"

"Switching now, Major," Zulu called back, and Track watched as Baslovitch took the tank commander's seat and the controls of the T-72.

Track worked the hatch control and threw the cover up. Putting himself over the rim, he could see men fleeing from the tank. Track climbed out on the turret now, avoiding the hot gun, and jumped to the ground. He looked back once and saw Zulu come over the hatchway and jump down beside him. "The rearmost building—come on!" Track shouted.

Track ran toward the smoldering ruins of the reception building, skirting it now and jumping the body of a dead Soviet special forces trooper, looking to right and left through the fire and smoke of the burning buildings, the burning trees, the debris, encountering no resistance.

Zulu beside him, Track shouted, "We've got to find Desiree and Diane and Sir Abner and George—they should all be in that residential building."

Track slowed as he reached the far end of the reception building, gunfire hammering toward him from the central building, the actual main research building.

Track tucked back, against the side wall of the reception building, Zulu behind him.

"If they guard that building, Major, they are doing it for a purpose."

"I don't give a shit—we'll go around them," and Track started running back the way he had come, to skirt the outside perimeter of the five smaller buildings to reach the one at the rear. Zulu ran beside him. Two squads of Soviet special forces troops living or dying was an issue totally immaterial to him now. He just kept running.

WITH CHESTERTON'S HELP, Desiree Goth had forced the occupants of the residential building—men and women, scientists and their spouses—out into the battle-torn cold of the night. There had been no one among them who even remotely resembled the photos of Diane and Robert Beegh.

Desiree and Chesterton were alone in the building now, except for George, who was somewhere, searching for them, they knew. Chesterton, crouched beside Desiree, whispered, "When he comes, we can't let him kill both of us. If you were to kill George, it would come between you and Dan. And he'll need you, more than ever I think. So I'll do it. When George finds us, you run for it, and I'll try reasoning with him. And if I can't, then—"

"There has to be another way. We can—"

"No, we can't. Our mission was to find Diane and her husband. We can't do that being pursued by an immensely strong, heavily armed man who is bent on homicide. He's not himself. And one of us has to make it out of here, to tell Dan that Robert Beegh isn't Robert Beegh at all."

"What?" Desiree asked.

"George's father was taken captive by this Morton Tillman and the KGB. For three years they used drugs to drain Robert Beegh's brain of every detail of his work and his personal life. Tillman already bore a strong resemblance to Beegh and was in the same field of research. He murdered Robert Beegh and took his place. That whole incident where they were supposedly killed was some sort of cover to get them behind the Iron Curtain. And there must be something big going on with the special forces troops ringing the central building. Something to do with mind control—I don't really know what. Dan has to be told. Morton Tillman has to be stopped."

As if punctuating Chesterton's words, there was a shouted threat from beyond the small alcove in which they hid.

"I know you are there," George Beegh said, his voice thick with menace.

It was too late for Desiree to run now. Chesterton stood in front of her, his pistol clamped in his right fist.

21

Dan Track skidded on his heels to the corner of the building nearest the living quarters. Fire still crackled from the buildings at the front of the compound. Track glanced at his watch. It had been four minutes since Zulu had announced that the apparent leader of the special-forces unit guarding the institute had been using a radio. If the man whom Baslovitch had identified as Colonel Dmitri Jurgenov had called up air support, it would be getting here any minute.

Track looked to Zulu. "We go in, through those back windows—blow 'em out."

"Quite. After you, Major," Zulu said, then smiled.

Track decided he'd have to remember that, Zulu smiling. It happened so rarely. If, that is, he would still be alive to remember it.

Track started forward, crossing the expanse of no-man's-land between the brick and stone buildings. Zulu was right behind him. The Soviet special forces detail posted around the central building started firing at them, and Track dived for shelter behind the near corner of a building. He pushed the

SPAS-12 around the corner, firing, jerking the trigger, emptying the magazine toward the Soviet troops as Zulu ran to join him. The Walther MPK subgun in Zulu's massive right fist was spitting fire in neat 3-round bursts.

Track tucked back as the black giant completed his juggernautlike run and was beside him. "Through those windows, Major?"

Track grinned at Zulu. "Quite."

"Indeed," Zulu said as he nodded, swapping magazines in the MPK. "After you again?"

"Right," Track rasped, feeding double O buck up the tube of the SPAS-12, working the magazine cut off, chambering a ninth round, then starting toward the windows. He fired the SPAS twice, once to his right, once to his left, the plate glass shattering inward in a shower of icicle-size spears. Track hurtled himself through the space.

He landed hard, going into a tuck roll, coming up, seeing no resistance in the long corridor ahead of him.

Ramming two more fresh rounds into the magazine tube, he ran ahead, hearing Zulu running behind him. . . .

"STAND BACK, GEORGE—whatever this man has told you, he's lying. He's not your father." Chesterton was gambling, Desiree thought. "He's using you against your friends," Chesterton continued, "against your uncle, even against your mother."

"You lying bastard!" George shouted back.

George raised the .45 in his right hand.

Sir Abner Chesterton replied by bringing his silenced pistol on line. "Don't make me shoot you, George, I'm your friend. Desiree is your friend. Don't—"

George lowered the .45, looking at it strangely, almost quizzically. "Sir Abner?" he asked.

"George!" Chesterton said. Dropping his gun to his side, he started to walk forward.

"Don't!" Desiree shrieked the word, trying to pull Chesterton back, but as Chesterton stepped forward, George's right arm rose suddenly and the pistol flashed forward, the slide and the front of the frame backhanding Chesterton across the right side of the head. Chesterton fell back, and Desiree grabbed the gun from the thigh holster under her skirt.

But George's hands found her, ripping the revolver from her grip. He threw her back against the wall, and in his eyes she saw something that terrified her. "George!" she shouted. "No!"

As George's massive left hand closed over her larynx, he raised the .45, the muzzle inches from her face. "He told me about you, too," he said, hatred rising in his voice. "You help the man who killed my uncle. My father knows all about you. Die, bitch!" The safety dropped with an audible click.

Desiree Goth stared death in the face down the muzzle of George's pistol. She slammed her right knee up into George's crotch and dug the nails of both hands into George's left wrist. George stepped back from her, his hand releasing the death grip on her throat for an instant as she slipped to the floor.

George swayed a moment, staring at his left wrist, then leveled the pistol at her face.

Then Desiree heard Dan Track's voice echo down the hallway. "George, what the fuck are you doing?"

The look in George's eyes changed from murder to insanity as he wheeled away from her.

Desiree looked past him. Dan Track, his SPAS-12 hanging on its sling at his side, stood at the far end of the reception area at the end of the corridor. Beside him, a Walther MPK submachine gun in his huge hands, was Zulu. She heard Zulu's voice then, "George, perhaps you are ill, but touch Miss Desiree and I'll cut you in half with this."

George answered, cold, machinelike. "I want him—then the rest of you." He raised his left arm, his left index finger extending. "I'm going to kill you!"

He was pointing to Dan Track.

"Zulu, stop him," Desiree shouted. "Dan won't—"

"No," Track yelled.

"Dan," she shot back. "Tillman isn't your brother-in-law. He murdered your brother-in-law and took his place. He's got George's mother here somewhere. He's given George drugs, and told him that you're the impostor. He thinks he's avenging your death, protecting his mother and father.''

Zulu stepped forward, the Walther in a hard assault position. ''I warn you, boy—step back, do nothing else.''

But George was still walking toward Dan Track. Desiree screamed, ''He almost beat Sir Abner to death, and tried choking me. He was going to shoot me, Dan!''

''Don't touch him,'' Track shouted.

''Dan!''

''Shut up,'' Track snapped. ''George,'' he began.

''I'm going to kill you!'' George said slowly and deliberately.

She watched as Track's fists clenched closed, then opened, ''Look—''

''No!'' George almost screamed.

Zulu stepped between Track and George, but Track shoved him away. ''Let him alone!''

''He'll kill you—or Desiree!''

''Let him alone!'' Then he said to George, ''You want to kill me? Fine. Let's see if you're man enough to do it with your hands, George. Or don't you have the guts to play it without guns?''

George raised the pistol in his right hand. Zulu braced, but Track never moved.

George threw the pistol onto the sofa cushions, then reached to the shoulder harness across his body, slipped it off and threw it down beside the .45. ''I'll rip you goddamned apart!''

"I'll get him now—" Zulu began.

"No!" Track shouted to Zulu.

Track shoved the SPAS-12 into Zulu's hand and set his handguns on the carpeted floor.

Track stood to his full height and started forward. George pulled off his Jack Daniels baseball cap and muttered, "I'm going to hammer the shit out of you, you son of a bitch!"

"Try it, boy," Track said.

They stopped, perhaps a yard apart. Desiree knelt on the floor, Sir Abner Chesterton's head in her lap, the right side of his face puffing, darkening, blood trickling from his forehead.

She looked to Dan Track and George Beegh, and she wept freely.

22

Dan Track, his voice hoarse, whispered, "No matter what, as long as I'm breathing, don't interfere, Zulu!"

"Major," Zulu said, "George outweighs you by at least fifty pounds, is eleven years your junior and several inches taller than you. And he wants to kill you. I assume you don't wish to even harm him."

"Just keep out of it," Track snarled. Track had never taken his eyes from George. He had guessed right—Tillman might have used drugs to control George's mind, but the basic personality hadn't changed. George had always preferred hand-to-hand combat over anything with weapons, prided himself on being able to pound, kick or stomp any adversary into the ground.

The drugs had not changed that.

George was moving right, Track moved right as well, and they moved in a circle, the distance between them less than a yard. George's hands slowly raised to a street fighter's wide-open boxing guard, wide-open for a purpose, to sucker the opponent. "Come on, George," Track taunted. "I taught you better than that. Remember, I grew up in the streets, too, kid.''

"Fuck you! You going to fight or talk?"

"Just like chess, boy—you got the white pieces, go for it!"

George feigned a left lead, changing his stance as he did. His right fist flared out and Track dodged it, but George's left tipped Track at the base of the chin. Track snapped his head back and away from it. George fought ambidextrously, changing from a right-guard stance to a left-guard stance at will. Track hadn't considered that.

"Caught me flat-footed—almost," Track snapped as George threw a roundhouse right. Track knew it was a fake, and saw George's left hammering toward his midsection. He sidestepped it, wheeling right, and kicked George in the rib cage, hammering the younger man back and away. Track finished the rotation, coming out of it in a kung fu stance.

Track looked across his right shoulder at George. "Come on, George—let's do it."

George hurled himself forward, Track sidestepping half right, the back of his right hand snaking out, crossing the bridge of George's nose—but not hard. George recovered, but Track's left elbow was already hacking upward against the right side of George's head. Then Track dodged back, but not fast enough.

The worst thing that could possibly happen had happened—George had a hand on him.

Track felt himself being pulled forward, off balance. George's right fist crossed toward his jaw, and Track snapped his head back and away but not fast enough. George's fist hammered rocklike against the left edge of Track's jawline. Track pushed his left knee up into George's abdomen, and elbowed him in the face.

Still George's left fist was knotted into the flesh and muscle of Track's right arm. Track threw his full body weight over George's left arm. Track's right elbow rocked back into George's solar plexus.

There was suddenly a horrible pain flooding over Track—it began at the top of his head and seemed to vibrate through his body. Track's hands were losing their grip, his knees weakening. There was another surge of pain near the base of his spine. As he tumbled forward he realized George had hammered his massive right fist down on the top of his head, then kneed the bone at the base of the spine.

Track's legs didn't respond for an instant as he fell face forward onto the carpeted floor, his head slamming hard against it.

He felt the pressure on his back, George's full body weight in a drop.

But then George's weight was gone, and Track rolled. He knew what would come next.

George never fought on the ground, always preferring to stand so he could use his feet.

Track didn't quite get away fast enough as he fled George's right foot, but it missed the side of his head and impacted against his chest instead.

Track rolled again, as George's left foot thundered toward his head. Track had full feeling back in his arms and legs now, and his arms and legs and his head ached maddeningly.

Track was backed against the sofa and he pushed himself up as George came at him again. George's left fist crashed down, and Track fell away from it, the coffee table Track fell on splintering under his weight.

Track jumped to his feet and edged around the sofa.

George suddenly jumped, planting his right foot into the couch, left foot on the back of the couch, the couch overturning, Track jumping back. Track heard Desiree scream, something she rarely did.

George's left hammered out, left-hooking Track on the right cheek. Track staggering back, and George closed for the kill.

Track let him come. To hold back would mean George would kill him. To avoid the possibility of injuring George would cost two lives, his own after George beat the life from him and George's when Zulu shot him to death.

George lunged forward as Track shoved himself away from the wall, floaters still passing across his eyes from the hard left to his head. But Track wheeled right, his left foot snapping out, kicking George in the chest, hammering him back.

Track shook his head to clear it.

Now was the moment. George rushed at him again, his left snapping out in short jabs, one connecting with Track's chin. Track backed off and launched a kick that caught George under the rib cage. But George's hands were on him again, on his throat, squeezing the life out of him.

Track's arms snapped up, both hands locking inside the crook of George's right elbow as Track twisted, feeling George's fingers gouging into his neck as he turned, both of Track's hands wrestling the elbow down, Track's right knee making a fast groin shot, Track stumbling back.

George hurtled forward again, as if the drugs somehow retarded pain as well. His hands were out for Track's throat, and Track ducked under them, planting a fast right in George's solar plexus, following it with another right, then a left. George sagged forward, and Track, behind him now, poised to kick George in the base of the spine, trying to immobilize the big man. But George turned and grabbed the ankle of Track's right leg in both hands and twisted. Track felt his balance go, and George threw him. Track went into a forward roll, and came up gasping for breath and cringing with pain. George was fast, strong and young.

As George came for him, Track dived forward, under George's hands. As he came up, he fully extended his right arm, and the middle knuckles of his fist punched into George's Adam's apple. George tottered back, and Track pushed the heel of his left hand into the base of George's chin. He followed this with a right fist to George's jaw. George's left hammered forward, and Track took it on the face and stumbled away.

Track pivoted, back-kicking into George's rib cage, then snapped his legs up again and delivered a full flying kick to George's chest, rocking him back. Track's feet touched the ground and he threw himself into a dead run, jumping, both feet ahead of him, landing in a full drop kick on George's chest. There would be no more fooling around.

George fell back, and Track kicked him hard on the side of the face. The young man's head snapped back, and Track launched another flying kick to the center of George's chest. George slammed into the wall, and sagged to the floor.

Track dropped to his left knee beside George, the base of his left hand at the base of George's nose, his right hand raised, the middle knuckle ready for a death blow to the Adam's apple that would collapse and crush George's windpipe, perhaps break his neck.

But Dan Track stopped his fist six inches from George's throat, then fell back on his haunches, rolling over onto his stomach, trying to catch his breath.

23

Strips of the fabric were cut from the couch with Zulu's knives, and George's hands and feet bound with them several times over. For insurance, Zulu twisted out one of the coil springs from the base of the couch and wound the heavy-gauge wire over the softer cloth bindings.

Track sat on another sofa, his head held between his knees. Beside him sat Chesterton, his face ashen and the cut on his forehead bleeding through an improvised bandage.

"So there you have it," Chesterton said.

Track looked up at Chesterton, then looked down at his watch. "Nine minutes. If that air support's coming, it'll be here in under three. Maybe sooner if there were birds in the air already. Special forces men or paratroopers could come in here and wipe the floor with us."

Track shook his head, thinking he was hallucinating. In front of him he saw Zulu, with seeming ease, hoist the unconscious George to his feet and sling him over his shoulder. "You know how much George weighs?" he asked the big black.

"I am experiencing that phenomenon, thank you, Major. Shall we?"

Zulu motioned with the Walther MPK he held in his left hand.

Track eased himself to his feet and cringed. His face hurt, his head ached worse than he had ever known it could ache. He picked up the SPAS, the rest of his weapons already back where they belonged. Chesterton had Zulu's SPAS, Desiree held George's .45 in her right fist, and her little 9mm Smith 469 in her left.

"All right, there's lots of guys with guns out there—no time to do anything fancy, we just go in." Track started ahead, forcing himself into a trot down the corridor leading to the far side of the residential building and the open breezeway. Outside, at least two dozen Soviet special forces personnel waited....

THE CORRIDOR was shaped like a wavy S. Track didn't stop to inspect any of the apartments that ran off it, but pushed ahead. Desiree was beside him, while Chesterton limped behind with Zulu, the big African showing the strain of carrying George's two hundred pounds plus on his right shoulder.

Ahead, Track could see the glass front of the building—what was left of it—and beyond, the Soviet troops.

Track pulled up and leaned his head back against the wall, closing his eyes. With the headache George had given him, it was hard to think. "PA system—is there a PA system here? Did we see one? I can't remember."

"Yes, I think so," Desiree said.

"All right, we've got Baslovitch with us and he should be able to hear in that tank you got us. He's on the far side of the compound with it. You and Sir Abner get into that PA system—one of you should be able to figure it out—and turn the speaker into a microphone. Get on it and tell Baslovitch to bring that tank up and get rid of these troopers for us."

"All right—what are you going to do?"

"Once the tank starts coming, I'm going right in with Zulu behind me and George on his back. We've got to get this Tillman asshole, get him to shoot George up with whatever it is that'll make him straight again. Then we've got to find Diane. Then I kill Tillman—and don't try and stop me. I'm just shooting the sucker dead, for what he did to Diane, for what he's done to George. Then that T-72 can blow this whole goddamned place to dust. Get going on that PA system—we don't have more than a couple of minutes, kid."

She leaned up to him and kissed him hard and full on the lips. Track folded his free left arm around her waist for a moment, leaning over her, then let her go. "Do that PA system," he said.

24

Sergei Baslovitch heard his name called over the PA system and he looked up. He had alternately been watching the few Soviet troops remaining in the front of the compound as they kept him under surveillance, and looking at his wristwatch. If an air strike had been called, he expected it to take place very soon.

He recognized Desiree Goth's voice. "Sergei— we need assistance at the center of the compound. There is heavy Soviet resistance. Hurry."

He had never killed the big diesel, and he started letting it run forward now, the tank shearing away part of what remained of one of the nearer building walls. Grenades were being tossed toward the T-72, and he could hear their impact, like hailstones. And with much the same effect.

A trooper fired an RPG. The missile made a terrible ringing sound when it hit the armor of the tank, but there was nothing he could do to avoid it. The RPG fired again, and Baslovitch kept the tank rolling.

When the flash was gone, so was the man who had launched the rocket. Baslovitch directed the tank toward the central building now, seeing the Soviet special forces personnel forming up against him through the viewer. If Track and the others were coming from the far side of the building, they should be in good shape by now, Baslovitch thought. The Russians seemed to be concentrating only on the tank.

TWO MEN GUARDED the doorway leading to the central building. Track shot out the rest of the glass in the window nearest him and jumped through, emptying the SPAS as the two Soviet troopers began firing their AKS-74 assault rifles. But they were just that split second too late, and they both died before they could squeeze off a second round.

Coming slowly, still hauling George, Track could see Zulu. Track shot out the glass remaining in the front doors and entered the building, his head pounding worse with each footfall.

He could hear the tank beyond the far side of the building, hear its heavy machine gun. Track shouted back to Zulu, "They're going to figure out there's only one man in that tank pretty damn quick. Let's head for the auditorium at the center of the building and fan out from there. Desiree and Sir Abner should be with us in a minute."

Track didn't wait for an answer, running the length of the short corridor toward the center of the structure, the SPAS at high port. If what Chesterton had said about seeing no other prisoners in the detention area was accurate, and if all of the prisoners were kept to be used for their mental abilities, however peculiar, then the only room in the complex big enough to hold any large number of people would be the auditorium.

Track skidded on his heels at the end of the corridor as automatic weapons fire hammered toward him. A fleeting glimpse of the guards showed they were institutional guards, not special forces. Track shifted the sling for the SPAS off his shoulders and grasped the crowd controller by the pistol grip, stabbing it around the corner, firing out half the magazine.

Automatic weapons fire chewed into the corridor wall at the level he had held the SPAS, and Track dived under it into the corridor, firing out the SPAS toward the two men. The nearer of the two men went down hard; the second man fell to his knees, wounded, still firing. The floor beside Track plowed up under the impact of the slugs, and he brought the Smith .357 into his right fist. He double-actioned the trigger, and the Soviet guard rocked with the impacts, his autorifle spitting out a final burst as he went down. Track felt a hot stab of pain in his left hand, and he pulled himself to his feet, jamming the empty revolver into his trouser band.

As he tucked back against the wall, Track wiped the blood away from a deep wound with a handkerchief. Using his right hand and his teeth, he twisted the bandanna around the wounded hand, knotting it in place. Blood oozed from both sides of the improvised bandage. He reached out quickly into the corridor and retrieved the SPAS, and began feeding fresh shot shells up the tube.

The tank still rumbled from beyond the auditorium, the thudding louder now. Soon the ammo would be gone. Soon the air strike would begin.

As he reslung the SPAS, and started to reload the Smith revolver, Zulu ran up beside him.

"The auditorium may be guarded," Zulu cautioned.

"Let's find out, huh?"

Again, Zulu smiled. "You have a flair for succinctness, Major."

Track started ahead slowly into the corridor. He heard noise behind him and wheeled toward it, only to see Desiree and Chesterton coming toward him.

Track peered around the corner. The auditorium seemed to be a rounded affair, with two large doors leading into it to their right.

"This is it," he said. "Sir Abner, you're more mobile than Zulu, so stick close. Back us up."

"Do what I can, Dan."

Track started for the double doors.

He stopped in front of them. He was about to confront his past, he could feel it inside him.

He took a step back and kicked open the doors, the doors flying inward as they parted.

Inside, the room was totally dark.

For a moment, he was unconscious of any

sound around him. Then he heard the chanting—
"I will warm them. I will warm them."

Track felt near the door frame and found a
light-switch bank. Then he hit all the switches with
the edge of his hand.

Sitting in the center of some twenty people
dressed in prison clothes, dressed as if she had
stepped from the pages of Vogue, was his dead
sister—alive.

Track aimed the SPAS-12 shotgun at the man
with the face of Robert Beegh, the man who had
taken his sister from him, turned George against
him. He didn't pull the trigger—he needed Morton Tillman to tell him things, and quickly.

Then he would either shoot him or kill him with
his bare hands.

25

"Dan! Why did you come back? To try to kill us again?"

Track watched his sister stare at him from the center of the group of people, a look of fear distorting her features. She was afraid of him, as he thought that if for nothing else, Tillman would have to pay for that.

"Do you really think George is dead?" he answered.

"Robert told me that he had somehow stayed alive. I helped to bring him here, but I haven't seen him."

"You saw him, Diane. I was there." Track looked at Chesterton.

"No, I—"

"Put him down, Zulu," Track ordered, and Zulu eased George Beegh to the floor, still trussed against the homicidal intent of the drugs.

"George! My God, what did—" Diane began.

"He tried to kill me, and almost killed this man," Track said, gesturing to Chesterton. "Morton Tillman is not your real husband. He isn't Robert—he killed Robert. Your system is all pumped up with drugs—that's why you didn't know George when you saw him. You have to decide, Diane, will you come with me?'' Dan Track set down the SPAS-12 and walked across the auditorium floor, threading his way down the aisle to the center of the knot of twenty people.

Track spread his arms to her. She stared back at him, still half afraid, but now beginning to wonder. ''Should I—'' she began.

''Remember,'' Track said, his throat very tight, ''remember—what the hell!'' He couldn't talk. He heard Desiree's voice from behind him.

''Diane, your brother told me all about your past. What he's trying to say—remember what your father said before they put the two of you aboard the lifeboat? Dan came here because of that. He promised to take care of you. Can't you believe in him?''

And Track felt Diane's hands touch fleetingly at his face. He looked into his sister's eyes. They were his eyes, George's eyes, their mother's eyes. And her eyes were tear-rimmed. ''Is this true?'' she asked.

''Yeah, all of it, sis.''

''I haven't been called that for—'' She sagged against him, Track holding her tight, letting the tears come as he kissed her forehead and held her tighter than he'd ever held anyone. It lasted a long time and what interrupted it was Zulu's voice.

Track looked up to see Zulu holding two Gerber Mark 2 fighting knives against Morton Tillman's temples. "George stirs from unconsciousness. Whatever drug you have given him, we need to know its nature and have its antidote. No doubt, Major Track may wish to kill you himself, but be that as it may, with these fine examples of the steelsmith's art I shall carve your meager being until you can no longer scream out in agony, but only divulge the information I seek by scrawling it with the stump of what was once a finger in your ruby-red blood. I will not talk, nor will I debate, nor is waiting in my plan. You will give us the information or I will commence my work."

Zulu began to move the knives, and Track felt Diane tense in his arms.

Morton Tillman, sweat beading his face, blurted out, "The drug will wear off in about another hour. You can accelerate the process with ordinary aspirin. The antiinflammatory agents help to clear the residue of the drug from the bloodstream."

"There's aspirin in the medical chest, I think." Diane pointed toward the wall of the auditorium behind them.

Desiree ran for the medical chest mounted near the double doors.

Chesterton guarded the doorway with Zulu's MPK.

Zulu spoke again. "And for Diane?"

"There is nothing. She has a different drug—all of them do. It's for expanding the consciousness. It wears off but usually, I, ah—I give a sedative to sleep it off, and I give a version of the drug I gave George for controlling her—for controlling the others afterward.''

"What else?" Zulu demanded.

Tillman stared at the big African, saying nothing.

Zulu slashed the blade in his left hand across Tillman's cheek. Tillman screamed and Zulu rested the tip of the second blade underneath Tillman's chin. "It will be much harder later," he said.

"All right," Tillman said as he shrugged. "It won't do any of you any good. Okay, you stopped me and we didn't finish setting off the detonators in the missile silos near New York City. But my work is all here. Someone else can carry it on. We can use people to bring down aircraft, to incinerate men inside their tanks, to—"

"Enough!" Zulu shouted. "The drug—"

"They're all dying," Tillman replied with a smile. "And there's nothing you can do. The drug causes cancer in the cerebral cortex—I never knew why. But all of them, Diane most of all—most of all, Track—will die in agony within weeks and there's nothing you can do to stop that."

Track reached out with his hand, pushing Zulu away. Diane was screaming. But with his right hand, Daniel Hunter Track drew the Smith .357 Magnum and pointed it at Morton Tillman's face. With barely a hesitation, his index finger moved six times and Tillman's head exploded in a spray of blood and brain and bone. As the sound of the shots died away, the only movement came from the headless body that flapped like something inhuman on the auditorium floor.

26

The air strike would come at any second, and there would be several hundred Soviet special forces and airborne personnel flooding the base. He would go down with everyone he loved around him, Dan Track thought. Diane. George. Desiree. His friends, Zulu and Sir Abner Chesterton. After he had exterminated Morton Tillman, Zulu had turned to him and said nothing, but clapped his giant right hand on Track's left shoulder, then walked to the doors to assist Desiree with George. Desiree had come to Track, held him.

Diane sat with George's head cradled in her lap, rocking him as if he was still her infant.

"Perhaps I should get Baslovitch from the tank. We can all go together that way," Chesterton remarked at last.

"I had a helicopter ready to come in from China—Zulu has the signal device. But we'll never get away from their gunships," Desiree murmured. "And there was only room enough for George, Sir Abner, Zulu, Diane and one other. And you and I. We could get Baslovitch aboard, but these people—"

Desiree sat in one of the auditorium seats, Track sitting on the floor beside her, his head leaned back against her thighs, his eyes staring upward at the acoustical-tile ceiling two stories above. The auditorium was the reason for the second floor, Track thought absently, to give a sufficiently high ceiling.

"Yeah," Track rasped, answering Chesterton. "Get Baslovitch. We can all go together. That tank won't save our necks now." Track looked down from the ceiling, guillotining a cigar. He told Chesterton, "Have Sergei bring the tank near the doors at the end of the corridor. We can fire it out and get some of them, hide behind the tank when they come. At least we'll make them have us hard." He had already decided that Diane and Desiree would die at his hands—he didn't want to imagine what the KGB would do to them. And Baslovitch would be better off dead too, if it came to that.

Track cleared his eyes, a shiver running along his spine.

When he was a little boy, he had done something very dangerous once and his father had saved his life—he didn't even remember what it was. But he did remember his father saying that a brave man is more afraid than anyone, but a brave man doesn't only fight what it is he has to do, he fights the fear first in order to do it.

Dan Track lit his cigar, looking at the Zippo in his hands.

He could hear murmurings from George, and he looked over to see Diane and her son.

Dan Track stood up. "Diane, your people—" he began, staring at the twenty silent prisoners. Since he had entered the auditorium, none of them had spoken.

"Can we lead them up onto the roof of the building?" he continued. "Is there a way?"

"Yes, but why would we do that?"

"What that Tillman asshole said—"

"Of course, that's brilliant." It was Baslovitch's voice. Track looked up, and nodded to his Russian ally.

"You continually amaze me, Major," Zulu intoned. "Tillman has given us our weapon."

"Only if we can get up there in time to use it," Track answered.

"WOULD YOU LIKE me to tell you about those helicopters?" Sergei Baslovitch asked, pointing to the north.

Dan Track, the wind whipping across the roof, the moon bright, the air surrounding them cold, inhaled on his cigar, then nodded.

"Those are what your NATO people call the Hind-A. They carry a crew of four, and eight passengers in full battle gear. I make it about two dozen heading our way. That's nearly two hundred armed men who thoroughly dislike us by now. Each chopper carries one 12.7mm nose gun, four wire-guided antitank missiles, two off of each stub wing, and two additional missiles, rockets or pods on each wing. I doubt they'll use bombs or missiles though—they'd doubtless like as much as possible of the facility to remain intact."

Track looked down to the rooftop beside him. George sat there, looking dazed, propped between Desiree and Chesterton. George's body shook with the cold, and Track peeled off his bomber jacket and handed it to Desiree to place across George's shoulders.

Track's body still ached from the fight.

He looked back to Diane and her chorus of twenty mental sensitives. He could tell from her expression that her drugs were beginning to wear off, and without the drugs Morton Tillman had used, the pain from what was killing her was beginning to surface.

He listened as she spoke to her chorus. "There are men in those helicopters who wish to kill us, kill our friends, destroy all that is good in the world. We must destroy them. We must focus our minds to their fuel tanks, we must make their fuel tanks very warm, as warm as a fire. We must see fire in their fuel tanks. The warmth of fire. The warmth of fire. The warmth of fire," and like a chant again, another voice, then another, then another, chorused the words, "The warmth of fire."

Track turned away from them, and watched the sky, focusing on the running lights of the advancing helicopters.

The chant grew in intensity behind him. Suddenly, there was a brilliant flash of light in the sky, then another and another. The chanting continued to rise in strength, and Dan Track closed his eyes against the brilliant explosions of light in the dark sky. He heard Zulu murmur, "The mind is infinite, is it not? Our enemies wither and burn at its touch."

27

It had taken twenty minutes for the unmarked Chinese helicopter to arrive, and Zulu had had the pilot summon additional aircraft to ferry out Tillman's guinea pigs as well. Track, Desiree, George and Diane used the first machine. Already, the pain racked Diane's body.

Her death took two weeks. She had refused the painkillers that would dull her mind so that she could spend every waking moment with her son and with her brother.

She had told the Chinese all that she knew about Morton Tillman's experiments, and willingly submitted to their tests. American doctors had joined the Chinese doctors after the first three days. The knowledge of the evil Tillman had tried to bring into the world was now shared.

There was a hillside overlooking the place Diane Beegh had selected for her burial, and Dan Track, Desiree locked in his arms, the wind blowing hard, stood there now. George, Sir Abner Chesterton, Zulu and Sergei Baslovitch stood beside the fresh grave.

"When do you go?" Desiree whispered over the wind.

"Tomorrow."

"I'll help you, all of you. But you will come back to me. I know you will. No matter what the Russians do, no matter what the danger, you'll come back to me forever."

Dan Track folded her closer to him. With George Beegh, Sergei Baslovitch, Zulu and Sir Abner Chesterton, Dan Track would leave for Russia, to pay back to the Communist leadership many debts long overdue.

As he held Desiree, warm and alive in his arms, his mind could not release the image of the wind-blown grave site and the love that was lost to him forever there.

Debts, long overdue.

Track is Explosive!

GET THE NEW WAR BOOK AND MACK BOLAN BUMPER STICKER FREE!

Mail this coupon today!

1. How do you rate _____ ?
   (Please print book TITLE)

   1.6 ☐ excellent　　　.4 ☐ good　　　.2 ☐ not so good
   .5 ☐ very good　　　.3 ☐ fair　　　.1 ☐ poor

2. How likely are you to purchase another book in this series?
   2.1 ☐ definitely would purchase　　.2 ☐ probably would not purchase
   .2 ☐ probably would purchase　　.4 ☐ definitely would not purchase

3. How do you compare this book with similar books you usually read?
   3.1 ☐ far better than others　　.4 ☐ not as good
   .2 ☐ better than others　　.5 ☐ definitely not as good
   .3 ☐ about the same

4. Have you any additional comments about this book?
   _____ (4)
   _____ (6)

5. How did you *first* become aware of this book?
   8. ☐ read other books in series　　11. ☐ friend's recommendation
   9. ☐ in-store display　　12. ☐ ad inside other books
   10. ☐ TV, radio or magazine ad　　13. ☐ other _____
   　　　　　　　　　　　　　　　　　　　　　(please specify)

6. What *most* prompted you to buy this book?
   14. ☐ read other books in series　17. ☐ title　　20. ☐ story outline on back
   15. ☐ friend's recommendation　18. ☐ author　21. ☐ read a few pages
   16. ☐ picture on cover　19. ☐ advertising　22. ☐ other _____
   　　　　　　　　　　　　　　　　　　　　　　　(please specify)

7. Have you purchased any books from any of these series or by these authors in
   the past 12 months? Approximately how many?

	No. Purchased		No. Purchased
☐ Mack Bolan	(23) ____	☐ Clive Cussler	(49) ____
☐ Able Team	(25) ____	☐ Len Deighton	(51) ____
☐ Phoenix Force	(27) ____	☐ Ken Follet	(53) ____
☐ SOBs	(29) ____	☐ Colin Forbes	(55) ____
☐ Dagger	(31) ____	☐ Frederick Forsyth	(57) ____
☐ The Destroyer	(33) ____	☐ Adam Hall	(59) ____
☐ Death Merchant	(35) ____	☐ Jack Higgins	(61) ____
☐ Rat Bastards	(37) ____	☐ Gregory MacDonald	(63) ____
☐ Hawker	(39) ____	☐ John D. MacDonald	(65) ____
☐ Nick Carter	(41) ____	☐ Robert Ludlum	(67) ____
☐ The Survivalist	(43) ____	☐ Alistair MacLean	(69) ____
☐ Duncan Kyle	(45) ____	☐ John Gardner	(71) ____
☐ Stephen King	(47) ____	☐ Helen McInnes	(72) ____

8. On which date was this book purchased? (75) _____

9. Please indicate your age group and sex.
   77.1 ☐ Male　　78.1 ☐ under 15　.3 ☐ 25-34　.5 ☐ 50-64
   .2 ☐ Female　　.2 ☐ 15-24　.4 ☐ 35-49　.6 ☐ 65 or older

Thank you for completing and returning this questionnaire.

Printed in USA

P123456789

NAME _____
(Please Print)

ADDRESS _____

CITY _____

ZIP CODE _____

BUSINESS REPLY MAIL

FIRST CLASS   **PERMIT NO. 70**   **TEMPE, AZ.**

POSTAGE WILL BE PAID BY ADDRESSEE

NATIONAL READER SURVEYS

2504 West Southern Avenue
Tempe, AZ   85282